a novella

broken

the woman
who anointed Jesus's feet

a novella

broken

the woman
who anointed Jesus's feet

GOLDEN KEYES
PARSONS

WhiteFire
Publishing

This is a work of fiction. All characters and events portrayed in this novel are either fictitious or used fictitiously.

BROKEN: THE WOMAN WHO ANOINTED JESUS'S FEET

WhiteFire Publishing
13607 Bedford Rd NE
Cumberland, MD 21502

ISBN: 978-1-939023-16-2 (print)
        978-1-939023-17-9 (digital)

To women who might have felt trapped, or alone,
or who needed forgiveness or healing—
who felt as if no one cared, or even knew their names.
An encounter with Jesus turned women's lives around
then—
and meeting Him still does today.

Dear Reader,

This series about nameless women in Scripture has been in my heart for 30 years. I wrote the first book about the adulterous woman approximately that long ago. I was an amateur writer then and made many mistakes on the technical side of the craft, but the story was there. And I kept pitching the idea to publishers and editors, but at that time the popularity of biblical fiction was waning. Or more well-known authors had a series out there that was too similar. But the series wouldn't let me go. It seemed interesting to me that some of the major encounters Jesus had in his ministry were with women, and that those women were not even named in the accounts. However, they were important enough to be included in the canon.

In the meantime, I got a contract for another series, based on my family genealogy in 17th century France, the Darkness to Light series, and subsequently published a Civil War novel set in Texas, *His Steadfast Love*. One day via a writers loop I learned that WhiteFire Publishing was interested in biblical fiction. They bought the series and they are now reality.

I hope you will find touchstones in these stories that will ring true to you as a woman. Jesus broke many cultural and social mores of the day to relate to women—women who felt trapped by laws and tradition; those who needed forgiveness; some who had been abused.

I love to hear from my readers. You may contact me through my web site at www.goldenkeyesparsons.com or by email at golden@goldenkeyesparsons.com.

May the One who has our names engraved on the palm of His hand minister to you through these novellas.

Blessings,
Golden Keyes Parsons

Tirzah plucked a delicate fuchsia bougainvillea blossom from the burgeoning vine covering the wall beside the synagogue and threaded it into her hair. A woman to her right frowned and turned aside. Eyes. Eyes that recognized but turned away. Inquisitive eyes. Eyes darkened with judgment.

Tirzah ignored the rebuff and put a slender hand to her forehead to shield her eyes from the piercing rays of the midday sun. Jesus exited the synagogue surrounded by a cluster of learned men, the *tzitzit* on the corners of their blue and white prayer shawls swinging as they bobbed back and forth, whispering among themselves. People cleared a swath around Tirzah. *It doesn't matter—simply offers me a better view.*

Women drew their children to their sides. Sneering lips and snubs didn't faze her anymore. She had long ago calloused herself against them.

Word had spread through Capernaum that Jesus would be in the community this week. Curious, Tirzah managed to be across the street in front of the synagogue at the time she calculated the teaching would be finished. It had lasted longer than she'd anticipated, but still she lingered. She wanted to see what the hubbub was about.

His appearance did not match the rather spectacular rumors swirling around him of limbs healed, blind eyes

opened, and multitudes miraculously fed. The man was of average height, dark haired—what she could see peeking out from his prayer shawl—and had a dark beard. She expected someone with a more imposing presence—someone tall with broad shoulders and a booming voice. He did look strong and robust, but his voice was mellow and soft. She would not have noticed him in a crowd. His most arresting features were his eyes. When he smiled, they crinkled in an engaging manner. Was it amusement? No, it was more like kindness or forbearance, graciousness perhaps.

Simon, a Pharisee whom she knew well, questioned the teacher as the men paused outside the entrance of the synagogue. He gestured with his hands in short choppy movements which he was prone to do when agitated. Leave it to Simon to make his opinion known. She couldn't hear what it was that had upset him, but he obviously was disturbed. He turned from side to side, nodding to his colleagues as if by doing so he would garner their agreement. Some nodded. Some stroked their beards. Some simply stood quietly by and observed. Simon glanced at her but turned his eyes away quickly. She knew he saw her, but he gave no sign of recognition.

Jesus answered a few questions from the men gathered around him, then turned to leave. As he glanced across the narrow street in Tirzah's direction, he caught her eye and held her gaze, smiling at her. A spark of recognition passed between them, but how could that be? She'd never seen him before.

Later that evening Tirzah answered the familiar rap. She slid the latch aside and opened the door, smiling as

Simon stepped inside. He came to Tirzah's house on the same night every week, hung his cloak on the same peg beside the door, and sat at her table in the same chair. She had already poured his glass of wine.

But this evening Simon produced a bundle wrapped in a beautiful scarf of variegated colors—blues, magentas, and purples. He seemed almost giddy, chuckling as he gently set it on the wooden table.

"What is this?"

"It's for you." He gestured with his hand. "Open it."

She sat beside him and fingered the scarf without lifting the package. "This is beautiful in itself."

Simon touched the dimple in her cheek. "Not as beautiful as you." He motioned toward the parcel again. "Go on. Open it."

She lifted and almost dropped it as the weight shifted in her hand. "Oops. It's heavy." Tirzah unwound the scarf to reveal a white alabaster container. "Oh. How lovely." She held it up to the flame of the candle. The alabaster ewer seemed translucent as she turned it around in her hand.

"It holds very expensive ointment—however, not to be used to perfume your most desirable body." His gaze swept from the top of her head to her feet, his eyes beckoning her toward him. "It is an investment for you, or to be used for burial spices." He scratched his beard and shrugged his shoulder. "Not that you would need it anytime soon, but I worry about you. You have no one...no one to look after you."

Tirzah set the container down and teased Simon, chucking him underneath his chin, then sitting in his lap. She took his face in her hands and nuzzled his beard. The cinnamon fragrance of the cassia oil that he used on his skin filled her nostrils. "I thought you said you would look after me."

He cleared his throat, reached for the wine goblet and swirled the red liquid around in the cup while balancing Tirzah on his knee. "That I intend to do, but if something happens to me, then what?"

"I have Claudia."

"A lot of good that cripple is to you."

"Hush! She'll hear you. She's loved me and been more loyal to me than anyone else in my life, except my mother." She rose and rewrapped the container in the scarf. "Oh, well, no need to bother about me. I'm simply a toy to you—something that you play with when you are in the mood and then put away when you go home to your wife."

He grabbed for her arm. "You know you mean more to me than that. Haven't I been good to you?"

She spun away from him and set the package on a shelf above the table. "What did you think about the rabbi who taught in the synagogue today? The miracle maker. He's causing quite a stir."

Simon raised his cup and took a swallow. "I saw you. Why do you subject yourself to the sneers and comments?"

"I was curious. And I have just as much right to be on the street as anybody else." She set a bowl of fruit and cheese on the wooden table. A ripe pomegranate tumbled out of the bowl, and Simon caught it as it rolled toward the edge of the table.

"So what do you think about him?"

"Humph. What do I think about him?" Simon dug a nail into the skin of the fruit and tore it open. "Just a teacher. A good teacher, but just a teacher."

"People say he performs miracles."

"Exaggerations. Coincidences. I've never seen one, have you?" He grinned and, setting the pomegranate aside, pulled her down to his lap again. "I think I shall have a closer look at the man soon."

"What do you mean?" Tirzah twirled a lock of his hair around her finger, and kissed the lobe of his ear.

"Perhaps an invitation to dinner would be in order—in a few days."

Tirzah stared at Simon. In spite of the fact that he was older, he was still a handsome man. His dark hair sported very little gray, just around the temples. Gray eyes still flashed with amusement and alertness, not the bleary, watery eyes of many older men. And he was still strong and walked with a spring in his step.

Trailing her fingers over his chest, she snuggled into his embrace. She preferred older men. They were not always in such a hurry, and she somehow felt more secure with them...safe. Not that any of them would admit to their families or in public that they even knew who she was. Even Simon wouldn't acknowledge her in public. But he was kind to her, so she agreed to give him a regular night.

Tirzah heard Claudia's halting gait on the outside stairs going up to her quarters. Loyal Claudia. Tirzah was grateful for her friend, but she missed her mother. She thought of her often, although her childhood memories were not pleasant. The life Rhoda had provided for Tirzah was sometimes scary—dangerous even.

She got out the flask of wine she kept for Simon, but her mind drifted far away.

chapter 2

A candle flickered in the next room and cast eerie images on the ceiling. Tirzah watched the formless pictures on the wall to make sure they didn't come to life. Her little girl imagination was certain eyes watched her from the sinister shadows. She curled into a ball and pulled her thin blanket over her head. Sometimes pulling her legs against her chest helped her tummy ache. Sometimes stretching out and lying flat eased the pain. So she moved from one position to the other, but it still hurt.

Voices filtered through the curtain separating her room from her mother's. It wasn't a room in reality—simply an alcove. The voices rose and fell, interspersed with a chuckle here and there. Then the man's voice sounded angry. Tirzah's stomach twisted and cramped like it always did when she was scared or nervous.

She called to her mother, "Ima. Ima!"

The man's deep voice rumbled through the small house. "Tell that brat to shut up, or I'll do it for you." A rustling. "I didn't come here to have to deal with your whelp."

Her mother threw the curtain aside. "Tirzah! You must be quiet. No matter what you hear, you must remain quiet. I've told you that over and over."

"But, Ima, my tummy—"

"Your tummy is fine. I'll get you some milk." She turned her back and hurried away.

Tirzah peered through the curtain to see a rotund bald-headed man with a bushy beard reach for her mother as she walked past him. "Come back, my little dove."

Rhoda brushed his cheek with her hand as she hurried past him. "One moment." She quickly poured Tirzah a cup of milk and brought it to her. She spat out in a whisper, "Now, drink this, and go to sleep."

Tirzah drank the milk, however it only made the stomach ache worse. She threw it up on the floor beside her pallet, but she didn't dare disturb her mother again. Although she wiped it up the best she could with her blanket, she knew she would be in trouble the next morning.

Tirzah listened to the sounds in the night she had grown so accustomed to.

Curling up in a ball again, she squeezed her eyes shut tight. She would not live the life of her mother and her grandmother—selling themselves to men to make money, men who came and went. None of them ever stayed.

She desperately longed for a father. She stared at the shadows on the ceiling and dreamt of a daddy who would rescue her from her pre-destined life of misery. She had no idea who her father was. She didn't ever remember having a father. In her fantasies, he would protect her from the myriad of men who came to visit her mother. Perhaps one day one of these men would turn out to be the father she so desired. Perhaps one day one of these men would fall in love with her mother and marry her. Perhaps one day...

"Hel-lo. And who might you be?"

Tirzah peered up at the tall man who had just approached their house. She clutched her rag doll to

her chest, along with a handful of dates and cucumbers. Looking toward the front door and then back at the man, she couldn't decide whether to stay or run.

Rhoda's words rang in her ear. "Stay out of sight. Don't need you scaring customers off."

And Tirzah tried to do that most of the time. She would play in the back courtyard with her doll and their goat, entertaining herself. But today she had wandered out to the street when she heard dogs barking and making a commotion. A turned-over cart of fruits and vegetables was the culprit. Beggars, taking advantage of the situation, grabbed up as much produce as they could hold. She dropped her doll by the front door and scrambled to seize what she could too. Now she was caught.

He put out his hand. "You don't need to be afraid of me. I just came to see your mother." He looked beyond Tirzah toward the house. "Is she here?"

Tirzah nodded and pushed open the door for the nice man. He bent over and picked up a cucumber she had dropped. "I believe this is yours."

Tirzah felt her cheeks flush. She didn't answer him, but took the cucumber, dumped the contraband on the table, and ran outside to play again in the courtyard until the nice man left. On his way out, he did something none of the other men had done. He called "good-bye" to her from the window.

She peeked through the door into the darkened house. "May I come in now?"

Rhoda turned and held out her arms. Several coins lay on the table. "Come here, my sweet."

Tirzah hesitated and looked around the room. Her heart seemed to stop. It was a rare event for her mother to welcome her in an embrace. She ran to her and nestled in her arms.

"Look, my sweet, at all the coins Adam left us. This will buy food for a week."

Tirzah nodded. "He was a nice man. I hope he comes back."

Rhoda scoffed. "Probably not. He's very young." Then she smiled and brushed Tirzah's tangled hair out of her eyes. "But he *was* a nice man."

Adam did come back. In fact, he came regularly. And every time he came he brought Tirzah a gift—a small little something—like a piece of fruit or a flower, but it always made her feel special. He would stick the flower in her hair and say, "A pretty girl always needs to have a flower in her hair, especially a pretty girl with such a sweet dimple." Tirzah touched the indention on her cheek and blushed. It was just like her mother's, and it embarrassed her when others commented about it, but Adam was different. He always gave the dimple a brush with the backs of his fingers as his "hello" or "good-bye" gesture.

He plaited wildflowers into a crown one day and put it on her head. "A princess needs a crown," he said.

Another time he brought a puppy—a fuzzy ball of sand-colored fur with two eyes the color of gold blinking back at her. Rhoda was not happy, but gave in as her daughter begged to keep the puppy. Tirzah fell in love that day for the first time. She named him Sandy. Not very original, but Rhoda let Tirzah pick the name.

Perhaps it was the second time Tirzah had fallen love, for she was already in love with Adam.

He had come that day as darkness had settled over their little house, and Tirzah played with her doll in the alcove. She pretended she was a princess who had been captured by a dragon. She wore the plaited crown of now dry and brittle wildflowers. A king, by the name of Adam, would come and rescue her.

Rhoda scolded him. "You are spoiling her."

"She's but a child. What kind of life is this for her? You must find someplace else for her to grow up."

Rhoda's voice rose. "What do you know about having to raise a child? I do the best I can. She's mine and I... do...the...best..." She hesitated, chewing on the inside of her cheek, and looked out the small narrow window in the clay wall.

A chair squeaked across the floor. "I'm sorry. I didn't mean to upset you."

Tirzah peeked through the curtain to see Adam cradling her mother in his arms. "I simply think you ought to consider trying to find another situation for her. Living here with you and the...uh...work that you do, is not good for her. Dangerous even." He glanced toward the curtain, and Tirzah stepped back. "She's so pretty. And most of your customers are not as benevolent as I, wouldn't you say?"

Rhoda pushed away from Adam and glared at him. "If you're so concerned about Tirzah, why don't you take her and raise her yourself? You seem to have a special affinity for her."

Adam sat down. "I would if I could, Rhoda, but you know I'm not married. I travel all the time. And my parents...I couldn't offer her much better." He spread his hands out on the table. "Don't you have any relatives who would take her? A brother? An uncle?"

"No one. And your parents what? They wouldn't approve of a whore's child? Well, do they approve of you maintaining a whore?" She walked to the other side of the room. Tirzah couldn't see her anymore.

Adam winced. "Don't talk like that. That's not how I think of you." He fingered the cup of wine in front of him. "I'll admit that when I first came to you, that's all I was

looking for, but then I got to know you and Tirzah, and—"
He stood, walked up behind Rhoda and encircled her in
his arms. "I wish things were different. I wish you were…
free. I wish I could marry you."

Straining on her tiptoes, Tirzah gasped and stumbled
through the curtain. She ran to the pair and inserted
herself into their hug. "Would you, oh, would you, Adam?
Then we could be a real family?"

Rhoda and Adam laughed as they pulled her into their
embrace. Could they be a real family? They didn't answer
her then, but she received her answer cruelly a few months
later.

chapter 3

"How long have you known?" Rhoda's voice penetrated the midnight gloom.

"Not long."

Tirzah sat up when she heard Adam's voice. She hadn't heard him come in. She was excited—he hadn't been to see them in quite a while. But he never came this late. He always came in the early evening. The men she didn't like came late at night—the ones who didn't want their acquaintances to see them. The ones who picked her mother up off the street and came home with her. The ones who were drunk before they came. Their voices were always harsh and abrasive. Or sometimes it was almost silent when they came, except for the rustling noises. Then a clink of coins on the table and a shutting of the door. But with Adam it was different—most of the time.

Tirzah threw her blanket aside and started to run to him, but something in their voices stopped her. She knelt and pulled her curtain aside just enough to observe the couple sitting by the soft glow of a single candle. Their faces reflected the gloom of the dim light.

Rhoda sat at the table, leaning forward and resting her chin on the knuckles of one of her hands. Adam sat on the opposite side as he reached across the table and gripped her other hand. Her mother pulled away and stood. "Not that I'm surprised. I was expecting to hear this news—just not this soon. You had to have known for a long time this was coming." She wiped her eyes with a towel she plucked from a peg beside the clay oven.

"What about Tirzah? You're going to break her heart." She began to pace. "I knew this was going to happen. I should never have let you into our lives, especially Tirzah's." Her voice, thick with emotion, rose as she pointed to herself. "I...I can handle this, but Tirzah really thought you were going to marry us. Rescue us from this drudgery, from these men who come into our house night after night, and leave a few coins on the table so we can eat the next day. She plays 'princess' with her doll who is going to be rescued by a handsome king named Adam. Not a prince, mind you. She doesn't want a lover to rescue her. She wants a daddy—a king to rescue his little princess." She stopped and jabbed her finger in Adam's face. "And you! You put those ideas in her head. Making flower crowns for her—telling her a princess needs a crown."

"I never meant to deceive her, only to show her some attention and kindness."

"No, Adam. This was not kindness. This was deceit—beyond deceit. This was cruel. Dashed hopes bring the severest kind of cruelty. It's better never to have those hopes and dreams than to nurture them, only to have them shattered."

Adam stood. "Please, Rhoda, please understand there is nothing I can do about this arranged marriage."

"Has the *ketubah* been signed?"

"Next week."

Rhoda's demeanor suddenly changed. She sidled up to Adam, leaned against him and ran her fingers through his hair. "Well, there's nothing that says you can't continue to come see me, even after you marry, is there? Most of my customers are married men."

Tirzah stared wide-eyed at her mother's switch in behavior. Heat surged to her cheeks.

Adam took Rhoda's hands in his. "You know I'm not that kind of man. Once I sign the *ketubah,* I'll not see you again. I will honor and respect my wife and our marriage agreement."

"Oh! So the high and mighty Adam is suddenly a man of honor who is too righteous to visit his whore anymore."

"Rhoda, don't…" He dropped her hands and stepped back. "This was all a mistake. I should never have come here in the first place. I was a young man full of curiosity about women and bursting with sensual longings, so one night on a dare—"

"A dare! Is that all Tirzah and I were to you? An answer to a 'dare'?"

He nodded, almost imperceptibly. "In the beginning, but I really liked you, and then when I met Tirzah and got to know both of you, I couldn't stop myself from coming back. I never meant to deceive either of you—especially Tirzah."

Tirzah stepped through the curtain, hugging Sandy. "Adam?"

Yipping playfully, the puppy jumped out of her arms and ran toward the young man. He knelt and scooped him up, scratching the dog behind his ears. "Hey, boy."

Tirzah stood in front of her curtain, staring first at her mother then at Adam. "You're leaving us? You don't want to marry *us*? You're going to marry someone else?"

Adam set the dog on the floor and walked toward Tirzah with his arms outstretched. "Come here, Princess."

Tirzah jumped into his arms and encircled his waist with her legs. "Don't go, Adam. Don't leave us. You're the only one who has ever loved us." She broke into wrenching sobs as she laid her head in the crook of his neck.

Rhoda turned away and ground her fist against her mouth.

"We're going…going to be…be a family. You said we would."

Adam sat down with Tirzah on his lap. "No, Tirzah. I never said that."

"B…but you brought us gifts and took us for walks, just like a real daddy."

Adam looked at Rhoda, his brow twisted into a tormented quirk. She would not look at him. He took Tirzah's hand in his. "I am so sorry if you took that to mean that we were going to be a family. I love you and your mother. I really do, but this is a marriage that my family has arranged, and there's nothing I can do about it."

Tirzah sat in Adam's lap for several minutes not saying a word as he tried to soothe her, the silence interrupted only by her gasps.

"Please try to understand." His voice rasped, hoarse with emotion.

Finally she whispered, "Will you ever come to see us?"

Adam shook his head. "I will not be able to."

"Are you moving away?"

"I don't know. Perhaps." He shifted Tirzah's weight on his knees. "Probably."

"So this is the last time we will ever see you?"

He nodded. "I'm afraid so."

Tirzah put her arms around his neck again and gripped him, her tears flowing once more. "Then st…stay until morning. I want to sleep in your lap all night."

Adam looked at Rhoda, and she nodded her assent. "Remain right where you are, Princess…until morning." He smoothed her hair. "And always remember that's what you are. You are a princess, worthy of someone to rescue you one of these days."

"Stop it, Adam. No more fanciful ideas." Rhoda spat out the words.

"No, I won't stop it. She is a princess, and someone needs to plant the seed in her. She does not need to live like this. God doesn't intend for her to live like this."

"God! What does God have to do with people like us?" Rhoda threw up her hands. "I give up." She walked out into the night to the courtyard. "Pfft! God!"

Tirzah fell asleep eventually, and Adam rocked her until the rays of the morning sunrise began to angle through the narrow window. Rhoda had come back inside and lay sleeping at Adam's feet. Tirzah roused to a half-awakened state as he carried her to her pallet. She watched through sleepy eyes as he walked to Rhoda and kissed her on the forehead and slipped out the front door. As he closed it, Sandy began to bark.

Tirzah sat up, her heart banging against her chest. Adam was gone. She ran out the door in time to see him disappear around the corner. Picking up the dog, she dashed after him, tears running down her cheeks, as she screamed, "Adam! Adam! Don't leave us! Come back! Please come back!"

Early morning vendors, alarmed by her shrieks, stopped in their preparations for the day and stared at the child. Rhoda came out of the door and ran after Tirzah. She grabbed hold of her. "Stop it, Tirzah. He's gone."

Tirzah broke away from her mother and darted to the corner, only to see him disappear around a building, but not before she saw him look back and raise his hand in a slight wave. She dropped Sandy and continued to chase him. "Adam! Adam! Don't leave us! Please don't leave us!" She tripped and fell, skinning her knees. She tried to get back up but was too spent. Her screams turned to whispers as she knelt in the dust and sobbed. "Adam. Adam. Please don't le...leave. You can't leave...your princess." Sandy romped around her and licked her face.

Rhoda caught up with Tirzah, took hold of her arm, and pulled her up. Blood seeped through her tunic. "Now look what you've done. You've bloodied your knees. Come on, my sweet. Let's take care of this." She held her, sobbing, in her arms and retraced their steps to the house. Rhoda stared ahead, ignoring the curious neighbors, as a single tear trickled down her cheek. "Adam's gone, Tirzah. You might as well accept it."

chapter 4

"Adam?"

The young man turned and looked down at Tirzah. "My name's not Adam, but that's a cute puppy you have there, little girl."

A glimpse of dark eyes. A familiar mantle. The profile of a young man. Many times Tirzah was convinced she saw Adam in the marketplace, but the man always proved to be somebody else. Adam disappeared from their lives. True to his word, he never visited them again, but for a couple of years, at the crescent of the New Moon each month, a package arrived.

Rhoda grumbled every time the parcel showed up on their doorstep. "How can we forget him if he keeps sending gifts?" Nevertheless she would unwrap the package and scatter the coins on the table. Placing one between her teeth, she would bite it and nod. "At least he's still sending the real thing." She repeated the same statement every month.

In addition there would be a small gift for each of them. Tirzah's favorite of all was a small crown made from gold filament wound tight and braided into a circle. There was no note, but she knew it was for his princess.

When Rhoda saw the crown, she picked it up and started to toss it aside. If Tirzah hadn't been watching her mother remove the contents, she really believed

Rhoda would have thrown it away. "Hmmph. For his little princess, I assume."

"Ima!" Tirzah jumped up from her chair and grabbed for the glittering piece. "That's for me. Give it here."

Rhoda hid it behind her back as Tirzah dove for it. She held it above her head and laughed at her daughter's antics to get it. "Oh, here you are." She handed it to the girl. "It's not a real crown anyway."

"It is too." Tirzah ran to the window and held the crown up in the sunlight. Rays of sun sparkled and danced among the golden threads, casting prisms of light on the wall. "See how it sparkles." She placed it on her head. "How does it look?"

Rhoda looked up from the coins and the woven tapestry belt she was tying around her waist. "Ridiculous."

Tirzah's face fell. "I think your belt is beautiful."

Rhoda shook her head slowly and walked to her daughter. "Come here." She knelt and took Tirzah's face in her hands. "I'm sorry, Tirzah. I think your crown is beautiful too. I guess I'm still angry with Adam for putting such ideas in your head." 〜*25*

"I *am* a princess. And now I have a crown to prove it."

"Ach." Rhoda stood and dismissed her daughter with a wave of her hand and returned to the table to put the coins away.

As long as the parcels kept coming with the coins inside, Rhoda didn't have to invite as many men home at night. And Tirzah didn't have to stay in her room so much. She liked that. They could eat the evening meal together and play with Sandy out in the courtyard. But the gifts stopped coming monthly after a couple of years. A package would appear on their small doorstep every three or four months, then every six months, eventually they only came once a year. Rhoda went back to work. And

Tirzah stopped waiting by the front porch.

Tirzah looked at her reflection in the shimmering surface of her water pot. She set it down beside the well in the dust and waited for the water to calm. Then she leaned over and watched her reflection again. She stared at her eyes. *Is that me in there? Who am I anyway? I don't even know who my father is.* She turned and pulled her headpiece just a little ways down to reveal the unusual mahogany color of her hair in the sun. *I...I look pretty.* She stared a little longer. *What is to happen to me? Will I get married? Most girls my age are already betrothed. Who is going to want somebody like me for a wife—a whore's daughter?* She stood up abruptly and pulled her headpiece back over her hair, set the water jug on her head and turned toward the village. Sandy chased a yellow butterfly down the path in front of her. Rhoda usually fetched their water, but as Tirzah had gotten older, she did it more often for her mother. And this morning Rhoda was not feeling well.

Tirzah set the cumbersome water pot down outside the front step and pushed open the front door. "Ima?"

Rhoda sat on her bed, rocking back and forth, groaning.

Tirzah stood frozen in the doorway for a moment then rushed to her mother's side. "What's wrong, Mama?" She looked down as blood splashed on her feet, dripping from the bed. "Ima! What's happening?" Her hands shook uncontrollably. "Tell me what to do."

"There's nothing you can do. This will pass, but it may get bad...before...agghh!" Blood gushed from Rhoda's body as she doubled over in pain.

Tirzah got a clay bowl and put it beneath her mother

to catch the hemorrhaging. She grabbed a towel from the kitchen table and tried to wipe the slimy mess, but it seemed the more she wiped, the more blood her mother passed. All she managed to do was smear it around.

Rhoda fell back on the bed, barely conscious—her face sallow and white.

Tirzah got a clean rag and dipped it in the water jug. She cooled Rhoda's face with the damp cloth as her mother mumbled, "The baby. Take the baby…"

Baby? Tirzah stood and stared at the large clot her mother had just passed. She barely could make out the small, still form of a baby. She knelt beside the bed and tried to wipe the blood from the mass of tissue. She made out little fingers and toes, a mouth and a nose. It was a boy, but he had no breath. Holding the baby in one hand, she gently tapped his cheeks. "Please, baby, breathe. Please breathe." No response. He was so small. She'd never seen a baby this tiny. He grew cold as she held him. Wrapping him in the cloth and snuggling him in her arms, she willed the warmth of her body into his. She tried to warm him beside the fire that was barely flickering in the oven. But to no avail—the child was dead. Finally she set him aside and finished cleaning up the blood.

Was this how I was born? With my mother alone—no one to help her?

Her mother lay quietly now. She stirred and looked down at Tirzah as she finished cleaning. "I'm sorry you have had to tend to this, Tirzah."

She avoided her mother's eyes. "Why didn't you tell me you were with child? I didn't know."

"It wasn't for you to be concerned with. It just happens from time to time."

"Like when you had me? It 'just happened'?"

"No, of course not." Rhoda extended her hand, but

27

Tirzah leaned back out of her mother's reach.

Rhoda's voice was barely above a whisper. "I wanted you. I wanted a baby then. I thought if I had a child, I would have someone to truly love me. I wanted you very much." She closed her eyes. "But since that time I've tried to be very careful—cleansing myself thoroughly. Occasionally, however, I would become aware that I had possibly conceived, and I would get a potion from Widow Miriam. I would try to detect it early, and, if I did, the potion would take care of the problem. However, if I was too far along..." She moaned and massaged her stomach. "I didn't realize I was so far along this time."

"Take care of the problem?" Tirzah rose to her feet and picked up the tiny bundle. She uncovered the baby's face. "This problem? This was a little baby boy that you 'took care of,' Mother. A child. A precious baby..." She couldn't continue as tears trickled down her cheeks. "How could you be so cruel? I could have had a little brother."

"And who would have taken care of this little brother? I can barely take care of us."

"I would have taken care of him." Tirzah lowered her head and wept quietly. "I would gladly have taken care of him."

Rhoda leaned up on one elbow. "Wrap another cloth around him and get that clay box with the lid from the top shelf above the oven. Put the body in there and bury it beyond the courtyard wall." She sighed and rested back on her pillow with one arm over her eyes. "I need to rest."

Tirzah found some cloves from the kitchen and sprinkled them into the box. She didn't know exactly what to use, but she knew that dead bodies were prepared with spices for burial. Then she got some fragrant ointment and dribbled it over the body. As her mother instructed, she dug a shallow grave with a broken potsherd in the sand

28

behind their courtyard. Several graves had been dug in the sand around the courtyard, but Tirzah had never thought much about them before. How many of them were babies or children? *Were any of them...?* She couldn't even bring herself to ask the question. Something about this seemed very wrong. Shouldn't she get the rabbi? Not that she and her mother frequented the synagogue, but it just seemed there should be something more...more formal. Her tears fell on the top of the clay container-turned-into-a-coffin as she placed it into the ground and set stones on top of it so no animals could get to it. She finished by covering it with dirt. Sandy had followed her and, unlike his usual playful self, sat beside her and whined from time to time as she worked. When she finished she stood and stared at the tiny grave for a few moments, then threw the potsherd into the scrawny bushes nearby. "Let's go, Sandy. That's the best I can do."

The dog leapt up and dashed in front of her through the gate into the courtyard. He wanted to play, but Tirzah was not in a playful mood. Every few minutes she flung a stick for the dog to fetch from where she sat on a bench along the stone wall covered with bougainvillea. Reaching up, she plucked one to put in her hair, then she maneuvered through the thorns and snapped off a few branches to take inside to her mother. Her thoughts returned to earlier that morning when she asked herself, *Who am I?* She was once a tiny baby like the one she just buried. Why had she been allowed to live and this baby had not been given that option?

Rhoda never mentioned the incident again. And Tirzah didn't question her mother, but the birth and burial of her baby brother gave Tirzah even firmer resolve this would never happen to her. She would not ever be with child unless she married. And if she ever married and

carried a child within her, she would bring it forth and be the best mother any child ever had. If she ever married…

# chapter 5

Tirzah cracked the door open just enough to see who had knocked. It was late, and there was no moon in the sky on this hot, dark, smothering night. Sandy stood by her side.

"I'm looking for Rhoda." The man had a deep voice with a raspy edge to it, and he pushed slightly on the door. Tirzah raised her candle and held the door steady with her foot as her mother had taught her. The man smiled, revealing a mouth full of crooked teeth. "Are you Rhoda?"

"Rhoda is my mother, and she is ill." Tirzah pushed on the door.

The man stuck his foot between the door and the jamb, his gaze traveling up and down her. "Well, you're a cute little thing. You'll do."

Tirzah gasped and tried to close the door. The man howled as it slammed on his foot. He put his shoulder down and rammed his way in, sending her stumbling backward. She scrambled to pick up the candle she'd dropped. "Get out of here! I told you my mother is ill."

"And I said that you would do." He came toward Tirzah and grabbed the sleeve of her tunic, pulling her toward him. Sandy crouched and bared his teeth. "Call that mongrel off." He shoved Tirzah down on the floor and began tearing at her clothing. Sandy lunged at the man, barking and nipping at his ankles. The intruder kicked the

dog, sending it against the wall as the animal yelped.

"Stop it! Don't! I'm not a whore. Leave me alone!"

He sneered and chuckled. "Whore, daughter of a whore. Makes no difference. One's the same as the other."

Tirzah kicked and screamed, but he was much stronger than she. She turned her head to avoid his putrid breath as he tried to kiss her.

"Come on, little one. Don't you want to start learning your mother's profession?"

Tirzah's mind reeled back to Adam saying she was a princess and not to let anyone tell her any different. She thrust her foot into the man's abdomen. Sandy now circled the man, snarling.

"I'm…not…a whore! Get away from me!"

Tirzah thrust about for anything she could use as a weapon. Her hand lit on a pot sitting by the hearth. She grabbed it by the edge and cracked it over the man's head. He swore and lurched back, still holding on to her.

"Let go of her." Rhoda's firm voice broke through the chaos. She held a candle in one hand and a knife in the other. "If you came for me, that's one thing, but she's not for sale." She put the candle down on the table and steadied herself, pointing the knife straight at the man's gut. "Come here, Sandy." The dog came to Rhoda's side, growling and snarling at the man. "Now get out of here before I release this dog on you." She gestured with the knife toward the door.

The man stopped and staggered up, feeling his head where Tirzah had hit him. Blood seeped from the wound onto his mantle. He raised his other hand. "Now, now. No need to get so excited about this. I was just having a little fun with the young one there." He scoffed. "She's of age, isn't she? About thirteen or so? She needs to get broken in, don't you think? Double income, you know. And I like the young ones." His lecherous smile curdled her blood as he turned his gaze to Rhoda. "Looks to me like you won't be working much longer. Getting a bit old for this line of work in my opinion."

Rhoda stepped toward him. "Maybe so, but my daughter is destined for better things."

Tirzah stared at her mother, unaccustomed to hearing such words from her.

The man reached for the door. "Humph. A lofty ideal, but not very probable." He lifted the latch and, after glowering at the two women, went out into the night. Sandy barked incessantly at the door after the man left.

"Hush, Sandy." Rhoda slumped to the floor, breathing hard.

Tirzah got to her feet, her whole body trembling. She guided her mother to the bench at the table. "Sit down here."

33

"I was hoping he wouldn't realize how weak I was."

Tirzah kissed her mother's hand. "Thank you." She took the knife out of the other hand. "Thank you for rescuing me. That man was horrible. Had you ever...ever seen him before?"

"No, not that one." She laughed softly. "You gave him something to remember us by. He'll have a lump on his head for a few days." Rhoda leaned on her daughter's shoulder. "Take me back to my bed before I pass out on you. But latch the door first."

Tirzah rose and went to the door, quickly latching it. Sandy followed close by. Tirzah patted him and nuzzled his head. "You did good too, boy." She tested the latch twice to make sure it was secure.

After she got her mother settled in bed, Tirzah went to her room with Sandy as silent, nocturnal moments swam by the cloudy sky that hid the moon. She shed her

torn tunic and tossed it in the corner. She would never again wear it. Then she put on the only remaining one she owned. Dampening a cloth in her wash basin, she washed her face where the wiry beard of the disgusting stranger had scratched her face. But as hard as she scrubbed she couldn't get rid of his smell. She would never forget the smell of unwashed body and decaying teeth.

For the first time that night Tirzah experienced what her mother's life was truly like. Strange men mauling her. Men who only cared about what she provided to them for a few coins. She lay back on her bed and looked out the narrow window. *I will not follow in my mother's footsteps. I vow again I will never resort to that.* She got up and went to the shelf in her small alcove and removed the crown Adam had sent her. At that moment, the clouds parted and revealed the soft rays of a rising moon. The crown caught the lunar glow and glimmered in its cool light. She set it atop her head and adjusted it, then lay down very still and straight and went to sleep—her dreams filled with a king who would come and rescue her.

34

chapter 6

"Tirzah, we need to go to the market. Get the baskets and the wagon."

Tirzah and Sandy accompanied Rhoda to the marketplace as usual, although the scorns and whispers that came their way caused Tirzah's cheeks to burn with embarrassment. Rhoda seemed oblivious. But she heard every word, because she whispered under her breath. "If that old biddy only knew—her husband comes to visit me weekly." And "Huh! That priest acts so pious, and he was at our house just last night."

"It's not fair, Mama. Why do they treat us like that? We've not done anything to them."

"Just walk on by and ignore them. Hurry up. Let's finish." Rhoda stuffed peppers, onions, and dates into her basket and motioned for Tirzah to bring hers. Melons and pomegranates went into Tirzah's wagon.

Sandy romped from Tirzah's side and ran across the street and behind a vendor's cart. "Sandy! Come back here." Tirzah chased after the dog.

"Hey there. Where did you come from?" A girl about Tirzah's age, sitting in a chair underneath the awning of a vendor's bin, held Sandy in one arm. She peeked shyly from beneath her headdress. "Hello. Is this your dog?"

"Yes, I'm sorry. Was he bothering you?" Tirzah took Sandy from her.

"Oh, no. He's so cute. Friendly too."

"Too friendly, I'm afraid. His name is Sandy." Tirzah laughed as she set the dog on the ground, and he romped back toward Rhoda. "What's your name? I don't think I've ever seen you around here before."

The girl held her arm folded across her chest. "No, I...I just came last week to live with my aunt and uncle. I don't...I don't know anybody here. My name is Claudia."

Claudia...lame. Tirzah stared at the girl's arm covering where the other arm should have been. The sleeve in the cloak hung loose. Claudia remained seated as her headdress slipped back and the girl struggled to pull it back over her hair with one hand.

"My name is Tirzah. How old are you?"

"Twelve, almost thirteen."

"So am I. And I would like to be your friend." *Why did I say that? Maybe she doesn't want to be my friend. Nobody else does.*

"You...you would?"

"I would. I don't have any friends, except Sandy, that is."

"I...I don't either...have any other friends, that is."

Tirzah knelt down beside Claudia and patted the dog who had returned to her side. "People don't allow their children to play with me."

"Why not?"

Tirzah leaned in and whispered. "My mother is a whore."

"Oh."

A long, embarrassed silence hung in the air between the two girls. Claudia slowly drew back her cloak, exposing a withered hand, turned inward and useless against her body. "Most our age don't want to play with me. My hand and foot are crippled. You may not want to either."

36

Tirzah stared at the deformed limb. "Yes, yes, I would. We can play in our courtyard, just over there." Tirzah stood and pointed to their house down the street. "And nobody would bother us there." Tirzah looked down at her new friend's feet. "Can you walk that far?"

"I can, but it's embarrassing. People stare and whisper about me."

"They do the same to me. That's why I don't come outside our courtyard very often." Tirzah pointed to her wagon. "I know what we can do. My wagon is big enough for you. You could sit in the wagon, and I could pull you to my house. It's not very far."

"What if people stare at us?"

"So what if they do? We'll stare back."

Claudia covered her mouth with her good hand and giggled.

Tirzah chuckled with her. "Wait here. I'll go empty the wagon. Can you come to my house now?"

"I'll ask." The girl rose and steadied herself with her good hand on the back of the chair. Claudia limped with a stiff up-and-down movement to the back of the vendor's cart where her aunt was bent over a cart of melons sorting and arranging them. She whispered in her aunt's ear. The woman looked over her shoulder at Tirzah for a long moment, then shook her head. Claudia whispered again, and her aunt turned and motioned for Tirzah to come to her.

Tirzah's heart raced in her chest. *What if she's going to scold me? What if she won't let Claudia be my friend?* She stooped and picked Sandy up in her arms and approached Claudia and her aunt. The woman looked at Tirzah with soft brown eyes, and when she smiled at her, Tirzah thought it the kindest smile she'd ever seen.

"What's your name?" The woman's voice was mellow

and inviting.

"Tirzah." Sandy struggled to get down, but she held on to him, keeping him between her and the woman.

"Where do you live?"

Tirzah pointed to their house a few doors down from where they stood. "The one with the painted door and the courtyard in back." Sandy got loose and jumped down but stayed by Tirzah's side.

"Hmm." The lady looked in the direction Tirzah had pointed. "Do you have your parents' permission to invite someone to come and play for the afternoon?"

"It's only my mother and me. I'm sure she won't mind. And I can wheel Claudia to my house in my wagon. See, there's my mother over there with the wagon."

"Oh, I see." The woman returned to straightening her wares. "Well, perhaps we could do that someday, but for now, how would you like to play here at our house behind our store? I think Claudia would be more comfortable here."

"Oh. I didn't think about that. Let me go ask my mother." She beckoned to Sandy. "C'mon, boy. Let's go." Turning to Claudia she said, "I'll be right back. I'm sure it will be fine."

Claudia's eyes lit up as she smiled. "I'll be here."

Tirzah ran to her mother, who was filling up the wagon with a variety of melons. "Who is that you were talking to?"

"Mother. I've made a friend. And she wants me to come to her house to play."

Rhoda didn't hesitate. "No."

"What? Why not? She's ever so nice."

"People like us don't have friends."

"But she doesn't have any friends, either. Mother, please. She really wants to be my friend."

"Why doesn't she have any friends?"

"Come. I'll show you." The two put their baskets of produce into the wagon on top of the melons and walked to Claudia's family's vendor's cart. Claudia's aunt came forward as they approached, with Claudia limping alongside her.

Rhoda whispered. "Ohh." She stood facing Claudia's aunt. "I'm Rhoda, Tirzah's mother."

"Yes, I know who you are." The woman wiped her hands on a towel. "I am Dorcas, Claudia's aunt." She smiled. "Tirzah is welcome to play here at our place with Claudia."

"Hmm. Are you certain it will not be a...a problem?" Rhoda glanced around. "She doesn't have many playmates."

"Neither does Claudia." Her kind voice flowed like honey over Tirzah. "I think they will find good companionship with each other."

Rhoda put her hand on Tirzah's shoulder. "Very well. Tirzah, help me carry the groceries home and you may come back and play for a while."

Tirzah jumped up and down, joyfully clapping her hands. "Thank you, thank you, Mother." She touched Claudia on the shoulder. "Don't go away. I shall be back quicker than you can imagine."

Claudia giggled again. "I'm not going anywhere. I'll wait for you right there." She pointed with her good hand to the chair where Tirzah had first seen her. "Hurry, and be sure to bring Sandy with you."

The two girls were inseparable from that day forward, united by their handicaps—one crippled in spirit and one crippled in body.

chapter 7

Tirzah and Claudia talked and giggled late into the night at Claudia's house and many nights thereafter.

Claudia's uncle Rueben complained when Tirzah came to play with her. "Why do those two always come to our house? Can't they play somewhere else? It's bad for business."

"Tell me, where do you want them to go? A sweet little girl that no one will have anything to do with because her mother is a harlot, and a cripple? Tell me, tell me— where?" Dorcas's soft, fluid voice escalated to an unheard-before pitch.

"I don't know, just not here." The man muttered under his breath and stalked off to wait on a customer.

Eventually they settled into a pattern of playing in the courtyard behind Rhoda and Tirzah's house during the day and then spending the nights at Claudia's. The problem of interfering with business was solved—both Rhoda's and Rueben's.

One sweltering night Tirzah tossed the blanket aside. "Aren't you hot? I'm sweating."

"No, not really. I'm always kind of cool at night." Claudia's voice, much like Dorcas's, was soft and unassuming.

"Are you really cool at night or do you not want me to see your arm? It's dark, and I wouldn't be able to see it anyway." Tirzah had waited several weeks for an opportunity to broach the subject of Claudia's infirmity.

Tirzah heard Claudia inhale sharply. "I...I don't know. I guess I never thought about it."

"How did it happen? I mean, were you born this way or was it some kind of accident?"

"I was born this way." She shifted so her good side was toward Tirzah. "I am the oldest of seven. All the rest are boys. My parents didn't know what to do with me, so my mother's sister, Aunt Dorcas, who has no children of her own, offered to let me live with them." She sniffled. "Ima and Abba just didn't want to have to deal with a cripple."

Tirzah reached across the pallet in the moonlight and uncovered Claudia's deformed hand. "You know, it doesn't matter to me what your arm looks like. I know it's not normal. But there's no reason to hide it from me. Besides, wouldn't it feel good just to be able to be free around someone and not be trying to hide all the time?"

"I guess so."

Tirzah replaced the blanket. "Well, keep this on it if you are cool, but if you're hot, toss it off and be comfortable. Now I'm going to sleep."

Tirzah turned over and closed her eyes. Soon she felt Claudia push the blanket down to the end of the pallet.

"What about you, Tirzah?" Claudia's soft voice roused Tirzah from her descent into slumber. She turned toward Claudia and leaned on one elbow. "What do you mean? What about me?"

Claudia sat up, her good arm clutching her crippled arm. "Well, my deformity is plain for everybody to see. People avoid me because they think I'm unclean. But what about you? People avoid you and call you unclean, but you haven't anything wrong with you. And you haven't done anything wrong. That has to hurt."

Tirzah lay back with her arms behind her head. "I'm used to it."

Neither girl said anything for a few moments. Claudia whispered, "I don't believe you." She hesitated. "Do you believe in God?"

"I don't know. He seems awfully far away. I don't think he really cares about little people like us."

"It doesn't matter to me that your mother is a harlot. There's no reason to pretend around me. Wouldn't it feel good for you to stop pretending and feel free around someone?"

Tirzah smiled. "Mimic."

Claudia turned over. "Good night. See you in the morning."

Tirzah couldn't go to sleep, but Claudia's heavy breathing signaled that her friend had drifted off. She'd never had a friend before, unless Sandy counted, but he couldn't talk back to her like Claudia. There had been Adam, but he wasn't really her friend, he was Rhoda's friend—and he left them. Claudia loved her for who she was, or in spite of who she was. Tirzah didn't really know which it was. But whichever way, she liked it. It felt good to have a friend.

"Do you ever think about getting married?" Tirzah had thought about it constantly the last few months. She and Claudia were both almost thirteen. Most of the girls their age in the village were already betrothed with plans to marry within the next couple of years.

"I try not to think about it. I know I shall never marry. No one wants a cripple."

Tirzah knew it was true, but she didn't want to make

her friend feel badly. "A smart boy would want you. You're the kindest, most patient, loving person I know. Not to mention beautiful."

"No, I'm not either—not beautiful anyway."

"Yes, you are. I'd give anything to have your clear complexion—and those eyes. They look right through one."

"Don't you think they are a strange color?"

"Different, yes, but in a good way." Tirzah smiled. "The color of your eyes is the same as my mother's copper pots."

"I have my mother's eyes, and I always thought she was beautiful." Claudia looked down. "Well, you are beautiful too. Your smile would make any boy melt. And that dimple is simply charming."

Tirzah touched her face and traced the crease of her dimple with her fingertips. "Oh, I think I'm attractive enough, but with no father to arrange a marriage and pay a dowry, no man will ever be interested in having me for his wife. Besides, no one wants the daughter of a harlot."

"What will we do, Tirzah, with no man to take care of us when our parents die? Sometimes I get frightened about what's going to happen to me." Fear threaded through Claudia's coppery eyes, making them flash gold.

Tirzah set her jaw. She balled her slender hand into a fist and hit the palm of her other hand with it. "I'll tell you what we're going to do. We are going take care of each other. Let's make a vow right now, a covenant, that we will never leave each other and will take care of each other until we die." Tirzah picked up a knife from the kitchen table and stretched out her hand. "Let's make a real covenant. I'll prick my finger to bring blood, and then I'll prick yours and we'll seal our vow with our blood."

Claudia drew back her good hand. "Ew, no. That will hurt."

43

broken

"No, it won't, silly. Just a little stick." She stuck the point of the knife in the tip of her finger like her mother did to get out a splinter. Dark, red blood formed a dot. "See, didn't hurt at all. Give me your hand."

Claudia held her hand toward Tirzah and squeezed her eyes shut. "Do it quickly." Tirzah pricked Claudia's finger. "Ow! That did too hurt!"

"Just a little." Tirzah smiled. "Now let's put our fingers together and vow always to live together and take care of each other...unless..."

"Unless what?"

"Well, unless one of us should happen to get married. But we'll still take care of the other one, even if one of us should get married. Whichever one of us gets married will make sure our husband understands that they have to take both of us."

"If one of us gets married, it will be you, Tirzah." Claudia's voice was very soft.

"I don't think so. But whatever might happen, we will take care of each other. Do you vow?"

"I vow."

Although they were young, Tirzah understood their vow carried within it the seed of a lifelong commitment. They needed each other in life...and in death.

44

Banging, hysterical cries, screams, more banging. At first Tirzah thought she was dreaming. She sat up in her bed as Sandy dashed to the front door, barking, barking, barking. No, she wasn't dreaming. Someone actually was at their front door. She didn't wait to put on her outer cloak, but rushed to the door in her tunic. Rhoda followed close behind.

A frantic Claudia, holding a small bundle in her good hand, stumbled into her friend's arms. "Aunt Dorcas. She... she's dead! I...I tried to awaken her, but...but she wouldn't wake up." She turned her tear-stained face toward Tirzah. "She's gone, Tirzah. She's gone. What am I to do now?"

Claudia didn't have to verbalize it. Tirzah knew she was asking if their vow they made with each other four years earlier was genuine. Rueben would turn her out. Would Tirzah take care of her now? She half-led, half-carried the crippled girl to a chair. Claudia set her bundle on the floor and put her head on Tirzah's shoulder and cried until Tirzah didn't know how she had any tears left.

"Had she been sick, Claudia? What happened?"

Claudia shook her head and wiped her tears with her sleeve. "No, but last night after we finished the evening meal she said she didn't feel well. She said she was light-headed and dizzy and was going to bed early. She...she simply didn't wake up this morning." Claudia's soft whimpering turned

into sobs. "I called to her and when she didn't answer, I bent over her and touched her shoulder…and…it…it was… she was cold, Tirzah. She was gone…and c–c–cold." The girl covered her mouth, but it didn't stop the wails. Tirzah held her and rocked her until her weeping finally subsided.

"Where is Rueben?"

"At the house. He told me to gather my…my belongings and get out. He said, 'Go to that whore's house and live there now. Nobody here wants you.' Then he s–said, 'Good riddance.' I did as he said and left." Tirzah held the girl tighter as she tried to subdue her sobs.

"Isn't there anyone else in the family who will wonder about you?"

"My parents, but they live so far away. And they gave me away once. Why would they want me back now?"

"Oh, dear." Rhoda folded her arms in front of her chest and paced slowly back and forth for a few moments. She stopped in front of the two girls with her hands on her hips. "Well, we will just do the best we can, won't we?"

Tirzah ran to her mother and hugged her. "Thank you, Mother."

"Ach!" Rhoda shrugged out of Tirzah's embrace and flicked her wrist at her. "What else can we do? Can't turn the child out."

Tirzah's little alcove barely held the two girls, now becoming women. In warm weather, they slept on the roof. One day Tirzah heard a commotion behind their courtyard. She peered over the wall of the roof and observed men dumping cedar posts behind their courtyard to be burned. She had an idea. She ran down the stairs into the courtyard. "Claudia, come with me."

"Wait on me. Where are we going?" Claudia followed Tirzah down the stairs at her own measured pace.

"I have an idea. I saw some men dragging cedar logs and dumping them in the back. We could use them to build a little lean-to on the roof to be our very own room."

"Do you know how to do that?"

"Well, not exactly, but together we can figure it out."

"What will your mother say?"

"I think she will be glad to get us out of the house… for her business." After all the years of dealing with it, Tirzah's cheeks still flushed with embarrassment when any reference to her mother's profession was mentioned.

"Oh, yes. I'm sure you are right." Claudia ducked her head. "I don't like being in the house when…I've never gotten used to all the men who come."

Tirzah shook her head. "I'm sorry."

She touched Tirzah's hand. "No, I'm sorry. I don't mean to embarrass you."

"I wish I could get over being embarrassed by it. It will never change." She took a deep breath. "Back to our project—we can use the outside stairs and never have to bother her. We can do everything for ourselves—cook here in the courtyard, do the laundry—all the chores we already perform. We'll simply sleep on the roof when the weather permits and not have to be in the house when mother has…guests."

They drug the logs up to the roof and fashioned a lean-to of sorts that blew over with the first strong wind that came along. But they learned how to make it sturdier and eventually had an adequate, serviceable addition to the home. Tirzah loved falling asleep under a moonlit sky. Claudia was a bit more hesitant and fearful at first, but grew to love it as well. Sandy stood guard and was their ever-constant companion.

The sweet, buttery fragrance of fresh bread baking floated from the loaves Tirzah pulled from the oven and filled her nostrils. She breathed it in and smiled. She didn't love the kneading necessary to make bread, but she loved the end result—crusty golden brown loaves with a soft doughy interior. She set the round loaves on the table, then put them into two baskets, one to take inside for her mother and one for her and Claudia upstairs. Their arrangement had worked well. The main problem they had was not new. Money was tight, and sometimes they didn't have enough food. Rhoda was getting older, and customers were not as plentiful. Tirzah tried not to think about what they would do when Rhoda couldn't bring in any money. Tirzah had sold bread in the marketplace, but it brought a pittance. Not nearly enough to support them—not even enough to pay the landlord. She would have to bake volumes more. That meant buying more flour.

Tirzah put the basket of bread on Rhoda's table. Her mother came into the room, her apron filled with tomatoes, squash, and melons. "Ah! Just in time. There's a round of cheese on the shelf for you as well."

"Thank you. Did you make some extra money?"

Rhoda smiled. "I did. And he's coming back tonight."

Tirzah stared at her mother's teeth. They were slowly rotting away, giving her a hag-like appearance. Would that happen to her teeth someday? Rhoda depended on her appearance to attract wealthy customers. What would happen when she no longer was attractive?

"A new customer?"

"Yes. A government official. Wealthy."

"That's good, huh?"

"Y-yes, I think so. I've heard he can be rough, but he was the perfect gentleman with me last night. Just rumors, I'm sure."

"Be careful, Mother."

"Always. No need to be fearful."

It was the thud against the wall that woke her up. No scream. No shout. Just a sickening thud. Tirzah jumped from her pallet and listened. She heard the front door close. Throwing on her cloak, she picked up a lantern and started down the stairs into the courtyard behind Sandy, who darted in front of her. She threw open the back door and ran into the dark room. "Mama! Are you all right? Mama?"

A groan came from somewhere near Rhoda's bed. Tirzah found her mother between the bed and the wall. Her face, bloody and battered, was already beginning to swell. Tirzah swung around, holding the light up; her trembling hand made the light dance on the walls. "Is he gone? Where is he?"

Her mother didn't answer her, simply groaned. A raspy rattle came out of her throat.

Claudia limped into the room. "What happened? Ohh, Rhoda."

"Here, help me get her up."

"No, just lay her down. I'll get a blanket and a damp cloth." Claudia brought the blanket and cloth and knelt down beside her friend. "Who did this?"

"I don't know. Someone Mama thought was going to be good to...to her." Tirzah lay her mother down beside the table and covered her with the blanket. She bathed the

blood from her face with the cool, wet cloth. Tirzah held Rhoda's hand. "Mama, speak to me. Who did this to you? Mama, Mama."

Rhoda took a deep breath rattling breath, her blank eyes staring up toward the ceiling.

Tirzah embraced her mother and screamed, "No, Ima! You can't leave us! Not yet! What are we going to do?" She cradled Rhoda's body and rocked back and forth. "Claudia, help me. What are we going to do?"

Claudia sat on the bench beside the table and stroked Tirzah's hair and cried with her. "I don't know, my friend. Perhaps God will make a way for us."

"Look at us. Has God made a way for us so far? I don't even know how I'm going to bury my mother." Tirzah lay her head on her mother's still chest and wept.

50~

Finally Tirzah wiped her tears away and stood. "The time for weeping is over." She and Claudia heated water and bathed Rhoda's body. Then Tirzah dressed her in the finest garment her mother owned—a white filmy cloak trimmed in gold that Adam had given her—and wrapped her in a blanket with her tapestry belt, a gift from Adam as well. Tirzah hadn't realized how thin her mother had become. Her bony shoulders protruded through the flimsy material. She looked so old.

Tirzah and Claudia had no idea how to properly prepare a dead body. They'd had no teaching or training. They had no one to help them. So as Tirzah had done for the little baby boy, she sprinkled some spices on top before they wrapped the blanket around her mother. They managed to drag Rhoda's body through the courtyard to the small burial ground behind it.

The burial was complete before dawn broke. Nobody saw. Nobody knew. A woman's life snuffed out, buried and gone, and nobody but two young women cared or even was aware. They sat on a bench in the courtyard, hugging each other and crying until the sun came up.

Tirzah pushed herself wearily up from the bench then helped her friend rise. "Let's clean up and try to get some sleep. Then we'll figure out what we are going to do."

Claudia stood and turned to go up the stairs to their

quarters.

Tirzah hesitated between the steps to the roof and the back door. "I suppose we can move in downstairs now."

Tears gathered in Claudia's eyes. "I suppose so."

A package arrived on the front doorstep a week after Rhoda died. Tirzah gasped and set it gingerly on the table. "It's from Adam."

"How do you know?"

"I just know. This is always how they come."

"Do you think he's heard about Rhoda?"

"How could he know? Nobody suspects. Mama wouldn't go out of the house for days at a time. Nobody will even miss her until the rent is due. No, this is just coincidence." Tirzah gazed at the package.

"Well, don't just stand there staring at it. Open it."

Tirzah untied the string with trembling fingers and unfolded the cloth to reveal a leather pouch. She took the pouch out of the wrapping and shook it. It sounded like coins. The leather drawstring wasn't simply tied, but was looped around the pouch several times then tied. It took her a few moments to untangle it. A pile of gold coins fell out along with a note.

> *I know it's been far too long since you have heard from me. My deepest apologies. My business travels have taken me to distant lands the last few years. My wife's brother is now handling that branch of our business, so I will not be gone as much. I hope you will forgive this rather impersonal gift, but if my calculations are correct, you may need funds for Tirzah's dowry. I hope this*

helps. I shall never forget the two of you.
Give my princess a hug. (Oh, and Sandy
too if he's still around.)

Love, Adam

Tirzah reached down and gave Sandy a pat on the head. "I thought he'd forgotten us."

Claudia touched the coins lying on the table. "It seems to me he cares for you a great deal." She looked at Tirzah, her eyes searching her friend's face. "I didn't know you could read."

"Adam taught me." Tirzah folded the note. "Do you know what this means? Because of Adam we have rent for several months now. Maybe we can figure out in the meantime what we need to do."

"Or maybe it means God is taking care of us."

Tirzah scoffed. "Believe what you want to."

The money Adam sent lasted for six months. Tirzah baked bread and took it to the market every morning. Claudia kept the house clean and did the cooking and laundry the best she could. But Tirzah soon realized she could not bake enough bread to feed them and keep their house.

"Claudia, do you think you could help me with the baking? We need almost twice as much as I'm able to bake."

"I'll try, but I'm simply not strong enough to do the kneading and rolling out the dough. Then lifting it out of the oven...I don't know. I think I'd be more of a hindrance than a help."

"I suppose we'll have to think of something else." Tirzah stood and paced in front of the oven. "I'll get bread

ready for market in the morning. Can you take charge of selling it tomorrow?"

"I think so. Where are you going?"

"I'm going to try to find Adam. He's got to be around here somewhere. If not in this town, a village close by. Otherwise he wouldn't have sent the money. He must be close by."

Claudia's eyes grew wide. "You cannot do that." Her usual soft voice took on an authoritative tone. "It's not safe. A young woman traveling alone—absolutely not. That is a crazy notion. Ask around the marketplace if you must, but you cannot go traipsing through the countryside by yourself, unescorted, looking for someone when you have no idea where he might be." She shook her head. "No. You will not do that."

Tirzah took a step back. "My goodness. I've never known you to voice your opinion that strongly about… about anything." She stared at her friend. Tears were brimming on the edge of Claudia's eyelids. The realization of what was truly in her friend's heart dawned on her. *She's frightened something will happen to me. Then she would have no one.*

"Very well." She patted Claudia's arm. "You're right. That was a foolish idea. We'll think of something else." She embraced Claudia and held her until her trembling ceased.

A few days later, Tirzah, carrying her empty basket, opened the door quietly and slipped into the house. "Claudia?" It was silent. Was she not here? "Claudia?" Where else would she be?

Tirzah went through the house to the courtyard. Not

there either. "Sandy. Come here, boy." No Sandy either.

Nothing cooking over the fire. For that matter, no fire. Tirzah's heart began to pound. This was not like Claudia. She returned to the front door and looked outside. Then she saw a familiar figure with the recognizable up-and-down gait coming down the street. Tirzah ran toward her, waving. "Claudia! Where have you been? I was worried." Sandy romped around Tirzah, jumping up on her.

The two women returned to their house arm in arm. "Now, where have you been? Did you bake some bread?" Tirzah stopped and looked at Claudia, who was fidgeting with her cloak. "What are you hiding in your cloak?"

"What? Why, nothing. Nothing at all."

"Come on. You've got something stuffed under your arm." Tirzah pulled on Claudia's cloak, and a beggar's cup fell out along with a few coins. "Claudia!"

Claudia's eyes filled with tears as she turned her back on Tirzah and covered her infirmity. "It's…it's all I can do to contribute. There's barely enough here to eat. I know there's no more flour to bake bread." She faced Tirzah, her lips pressed together as her chin shook. "We are on the verge of starving, Tirzah."

Tirzah sighed and sat down. "I know."

Claudia nodded and put the beggar's cup on the shelf. "We have no money and no food." She sat beside Tirzah. "I'm frightened. What's to become of us?"

"I will not go back on my vow to you. I will take care of you the best I can." Tirzah chewed on the inside of her cheek and inhaled deeply. "But there is a vow I'm going to have to rescind." A tear rolled down her cheek as she rose. "I need to bathe and dress." She started toward her mother's old room. "You may want to sleep on the roof tonight, Claudia."

55

Claudia's eyes darkened—colored by the realization of what Tirzah was saying. Her mouth tightened, as she pled with her friend. "Don't do this, Tirzah. We can find some other way."

"There is no other way. I'll be fine."

Claudia could not halt the tears that streamed down her cheeks as she covered her face with her good hand. "Don't, please don't." She looked at Tirzah through thick eyelashes that were matted with tears. "You don't have to do this. Surely there's some other way." She dissolved into silent weeping, shaking her head. "I cannot stand to think of you having to resort to…to this." She clutched at Tirzah's sleeve. "Please don't."

Tirzah took her friend's hand from her sleeve and pressed it. "Go on upstairs. Good night, my friend." Reluctantly Claudia turned and went out the door to climb the steps to the roof.

Sandy darted out to follow her. "Wait here, boy." Concerned that the dog would cause her friend to trip as he bounded up the steps, Tirzah listened to the clomp-clomp of Claudia's stilted gait until she got to the top. "Okay, boy, go on." Sandy looked up at her and whimpered. "Go on. It's fine now." The dog ran out the door and up the stairs. *I'm going to arrange to have a railing erected on those stairs—as soon as I can save some money.* She latched the door.

As soon as I make some money. If there were any other way, she wouldn't do this, but she didn't know how else to bring in enough. Her mother and grandmother endured it, and so could she.

Pulling a kettle from the hearth, she poured water into it and set it in the fireplace to heat. Then she went to her room and got her best cloak. Not that she had all that much to choose from. She had an everyday cloak and one that wasn't quite as worn. She would have to sew something more suitable for this kind of work, something more colorful and flashy. Spotting her mother's chest of things in the corner of the room, she opened the container and found a colorful scarf and veil that would add some interest, plus large gold earrings and multiple bangles and bracelets. Arranging the assortment on the bed, she stood back and looked. *Yes, that would do.*

The water had started to bubble. She poured the hot water into a basin, wet a cloth and washed. Tiptoeing to reach the top shelf of a cabinet beside oven, Tirzah moved dishes around until she found what she was looking for—a vial of Rhoda's perfumed oil. She shook it. Sloshing of the liquid let her know there was still some of the precious ointment left in the bottle. She removed the stopper and rubbed the oil all over her body. The heavy scent of henna filled the room, and with it memories of her mother flooded through her. Her knees grew weak, and she sat down on the bench beside the table.

The table where she and her mother had laughed, argued, and cried. The table where Adam shared meals with them. The table where men tossed their coins after they'd had their way with her.

Tirzah held her hands in front of her and watched them tremble. *I don't know if I can...can go through with this. I hated knowing what my mother was doing.* Gripping

her hands together, she willed them to stop. *At least I don't have a child to protect.*

Her breath caught in her throat as the possibility of such a thing hit her hard in the belly. *What if I get pregnant?* She pushed up from the table and shook her head, although there was no one in the room to see her, nor hear her. "I cannot allow that to happen." She hit the table with her fist. "I will not allow that to happen."

She returned to the room that had formerly been her mother's but was now hers. The lid on the chest containing her mother's things stood open. Tirzah knelt in front of it and dug through cloaks, veils, scarves, belts, and trinkets. There on the bottom lay the ugly bag her mother had used to cleanse herself. Tirzah slammed the lid and got up.

Sitting down at her mother's vanity, she picked up the bronze hand mirror and looked at her reflection. Rhoda's pots of cosmetics had remained untouched since she died. Tirzah took a small spatula and dipped it in the kohl. She spread some on her eye. *Too much. I'll have to learn how to do this.* She smeared it with her finger to tone it down. Then she opened a pot of red colored oil and applied it to her cheeks and lips. Her mahogany hair hung loose except for where she pinned it back on the sides with gold hair pins. Large dangling earrings completed the picture. Instead of her normal headpiece, she covered her head with a scarf made of blue silky fabric. It had been a gift from Adam.

Adam. *Forgive me, Adam. I know you would be disappointed in me.* She blinked back tears that threatened to smear her makeup. She patted her cheek and looked outside. It had grown dark. Time to go to work.

She stepped out the door and looked to the street corner. Her mother very seldom went beyond the corner so she could stay close to the house when Tirzah was alone. Was that all she had to do? Go stand on the street corner? She stepped out of the door and pulled it shut. Her sandaled feet made a shuffling sound as she made her way to the corner. She hugged the wall of the building and stayed in the shadows. A noise startled her and sent her heart pounding as she swirled around to Sandy's bark.

"Sandy! You scared me to death." She patted the dog on his head. "Go home, boy." He sat on his haunches and looked up at her, whimpering.

"Do you want to stay with me?" Kneeling beside him, she laughed and scratched behind his ears.

"Very well." She chuckled and rose to her feet. "That might not be a bad idea."

Night after night the young girl stood on the corner with the watchful dog. Sometimes the dog snarled and snapped, and the customer moved on. Sometimes the animal allowed the girl to take her customer home. But the loyal companion stayed by her side as she walked the streets like her mother and grandmother had done before her.

chapter 11

Tirzah poured Simon more wine. "So, what is your learned opinion, my pet? Is the man legitimate?"

"Who?"

"Jesus."

"Legitimate in what way?" Simon belched and set his cup of wine on the table. "He's a gifted teacher, that's obvious. A prophet? I doubt it."

"But what of the healings I've heard about, and the miraculous feedings?"

"Trickery. He's a charlatan."

"Must be pretty good at his trickery."

"Why do you say that?" Simon squirmed on the bench.

"I heard he has raised someone from the dead, before witnesses—a young man."

"There's no way we can be sure he was truly dead."

"They were on their way to bury him. He had on the burial garments. They were in the funeral procession for goodness sake." Tirzah laughed at Simon's uneasiness. "Why does that make you nervous, O righteous Pharisee? Wouldn't it be wonderful if this man can really work these miracles?"

"No one can raise someone from the dead except God—and that would be blasphemy." Simon stood and pulled Tirzah against his body. "Enough talk about this miracle worker. Work some miracles of your own here.

Show me what you can do." He rubbed against her. Although he'd recently developed a bit of a paunch, she could still feel his muscles as she caressed his arms. He whispered, "Umm, dance for me, little lady. I want to see you dance."

Tirzah began to sway and snap her fingers. "Sit down, my pet, and watch what this miracle worker can do." She stroked his cheek with her fingers and moved onto his lap. "I'll make ten years vanish off your life." She laughed and tugged on his cloak, removing it as she seduced him.

Tirzah put Simon's payment in the money jar on the shelf beside the alabaster jar. She bit down on one of the coins before she put the lid on the jar and smiled. She always thought of her mother when she did that. It was still early in the evening. Simon usually came early—like Adam had years ago. She went out to the courtyard to watch the sun set. She looked up on the roof. "Claudia?"

She heard Claudia clomp-clomping to the edge of the wall that encircled the rooftop. "Yes? Is Simon gone?"

"He's gone. Come on down. Let's eat outside tonight. It's cool and lovely in the courtyard."

"Be right there." The young woman came slowly down the steps with Sandy in front of her and hesitated beside the back door. "I have some lovely fruit inside. I'll be just a moment."

Tirzah smiled and followed her. "I'll help you. I'll get bread and cheese."

"I have fish as well that we can cook over the fire."

"Let's just eat the fruit and cheese with the bread. I'm not very hungry."

Claudia carried a large basket of oranges, grapes,

melons, dates, and figs to the table in the courtyard. Tirzah frowned at her pronounced limp.

"Is your leg bothering you?"

Claudia looked up and raised her eyebrows. "Why do you ask?"

"It seems to me that your limp is getting worse, and I simply wondered if you are in pain."

"Sometimes when the weather changes or when I've been sitting on the ground too long."

"Did you go out today—to the marketplace?"

Claudia looked down and clutched her bad arm. "Yes, for a little while."

"I told you that you don't have to do that anymore. I know you hate having to beg. With my regular customers, I'm making enough for both of us now." Tirzah touched her friend's shoulder. "How much did you get?"

"Enough for two days' worth of food." Claudia set wooden bowls down in front of them. "Please don't scold me. You have taken care of me so well. It makes me feel useful. And I know you hate having to do what you are doing to keep us fed and sheltered."

Tirzah shook her head. "We do what we have to. But begging is beneath you. You are useful to me here, keeping things in order." She munched on a piece of cheese. "Today I saw the man everyone is talking about. The one called Jesus who is supposedly a miracle worker."

"You did?" Claudia sat down and leaned toward Tirzah, her eyes wide. "What did he look like?"

"Very ordinary. Nice enough looking. Mesmerizing eyes. Kind." Tirzah popped a grape into her mouth. "Did you hear the rumor that he raised a young man from the dead?"

"No. Did he really?"

"There were many witnesses. I don't know how one

would fake that." Tirzah looked at Claudia. "I think it's worth a try."

"What is worth a try?"

"Give me your hands."

Claudia extended her good arm.

"Both of them."

Claudia looked down and pulled her crippled arm from her cloak. Tirzah took hold of both of Claudia's hands and caressed her fingers, the twisted ones and the straight ones. "What if…just what if this miracle worker could heal your infirmity? You could be whole and healthy—and maybe even get married." She kissed both of Claudia's hands and let go of them.

Claudia drew her bad hand into the dark folds of her cloak to its usual hiding place. "I…I don't know."

"What are you afraid of?"

"What if he is a counterfeit? What if he can't really heal?"

Tirzah stood and put her hands on her hips. "What if he can't? Would you be any worse off than you were before?"

"Well, I suppose not." Claudia pulled the basket of fruit toward her and struggled to her feet.

"Don't. Don't leave. Let's talk about this." She touched Claudia on the arm. "I hear he's healing all kinds of diseases and infirmities—blindness, leprosy, withered limbs, and now he's brought a dead man back to life." Tirzah took Claudia by the shoulders. "Wouldn't that be wonderful? You could run and jump and walk like a normal person. Your leg wouldn't hurt you anymore. You would no longer have to beg."

Claudia avoided Tirzah's gaze. "I wouldn't know how to act. I wouldn't know who I was. I've always been this way. I'm blessed that my parents didn't let me starve to

broken

death or didn't just put me out beside the road." Then she stared directly at Tirzah. "And what about you? How can I help you if I can't beg anymore?"

Tirzah threw back her head and laughed. "By marrying the richest man in town."

"We don't know that would happen."

Tirzah brushed from Claudia's eyes the tears that had just spilled out. Then she brushed her own away. "Please, dear one. Let's try. Let's find Jesus tomorrow and let's try. I vowed I would always take care of you the best way I knew how. Well, this is taking care of you the best way I know how."

Claudia began clearing the wooden table. "Very well. Tomorrow."

"Go on to bed. I'll get this." Tirzah hugged Claudia and watched her go up to the roof. She was always concerned about Claudia falling on the steps. Tirzah gathered the dishes and bowls of food and went inside. Sandy followed her and curled up in front of the hearth. She covered the leftover food, brushed off the table and went into her room. She didn't want to go out on the street tonight. She lit a lantern and tossed her outer garment on her bed. The gold crown that Adam had sent her when she was a little girl hung on the wall beside her vanity table. She took it down and placed it on her head. Princess. He had really made her feel like a princess then. *What a joke. Look at me now. A harlot, just like my mother and grandmother.* She untangled her hair from the gold filament, took off the crown, and rehung it on the wall.

She blew out the lantern and lay back on her pillow. Sandy sauntered into the room and jumped on the bed. Tirzah rubbed behind his ears. She closed her eyes, but her mind raced with what was planned for tomorrow. She and Claudia would go to the synagogue first and see if Jesus was coming there again. Then they would follow him. People were always following him around, she'd heard. Her thoughts drifted into the dream world between sleep and wakefulness.

Claudia was walking, normally, with a handsome young man. She carried a heart-shaped box in her hand, and they were laughing. They turned toward her, and she realized the young man was Adam. He took the heart-shaped box and extended it to her. Then Adam was Jesus. He looked at her and said, "I healed Claudia, and I can heal you too—if that's what you want."

She attempted to take the heart from him, but it remained out of her reach. Silent words formed within her. "I know you can heal a withered limb. But can you heal a withered heart?"

chapter 12

Tirzah woke up to Sandy licking her face. Throwing back the covers, she jumped from her bed. She splashed water on her face from the ewer on her vanity table and went to the back door as she unbraided her hair. The sun was well up, but she hadn't heard Claudia stirring. The young woman usually came into the kitchen before Tirzah arose every morning.

"Claudia?" Tirzah called up to her friend.

"Yes?" Tirzah could barely hear her.

Sandy ran up the stairs in front of Tirzah. "Are you ill?" She spotted her friend sitting in a chair overlooking the village.

"No, I'm not ill. I watched the sunrise this morning. It was really very lovely. But when I tried to get up…"

Tirzah rushed to her side. "What? What happened? Did you fall?"

"No, I…I didn't fall. I just can't seem to get up." She scooted to the edge of the chair. "You know last night when you asked if my bad leg was paining me? Well, it's not my bad leg that is bothering me. It's my 'good' leg. It seems to be getting weaker and weaker. I don't have the strength to push myself up."

"Here, let me help you." Tirzah put Claudia's arm around her shoulder and pulled her up. "There we go." She adjusted her weight. "Can you walk?"

"Maybe if I had a cane or a crutch I could manage."

"We won't need one. We're going to find that man today—that man, Jesus. He's going to heal you today."

"How are you going to get me there?"

"I know exactly how—the wagon. I'll take you in the wagon."

Claudia shook her head. "No, that's embarrassing. That's how you used to cart me around when we were little girls."

"We've always done what we need to do to survive. I'll do what we need to do to get you to Jesus. I'll help you get ready, then get you down the steps." Tirzah looked around. "You don't need to be trying to maneuver those steps anyway. I'll move up here."

"But if Jesus heals me, that won't be necessary, will it?"

"Hmm, you're right." They both chuckled. Tirzah led Claudia to her little lean-to room to prepare for the day. "What do you want to wear?"

Claudia pointed to a rust-colored cloak. "That one, but I need to ask you to help me with something else that's embarrassing."

Tirzah sat Claudia on the edge of her bed and knelt in front of her. "What's that?"

"I...I need to..." Claudia pointed underneath the bed to the chamber pot.

"Oh, of course." Tirzah helped her friend with her most private issues and felt the weakness and trembling of the young woman's body. Tirzah was alarmed at Claudia's sudden decline. Or perhaps it wasn't sudden. Maybe it had been happening slowly, and Tirzah simply hadn't noticed.

Tirzah assisted Claudia in dressing and managed to get her downstairs. She sat her at the table. "Here's bread and honey, and water. Just sit there until I get dressed. If you need something, I'm right here." She replaced a lock

of hair behind Claudia's ear and kissed her on the cheek. "Don't move. Promise?"

Claudia nodded and smiled. "I promise." She broke off a piece of bread. "You're too good to me."

Tirzah flicked her wrist. "Pfft! You can pay me back one of these days—after you marry that handsome, wealthy man."

"The wagon seemed so big when we were little girls. Now I barely fit into it."

The morning was nearly gone by the time Tirzah pulled the wagon around to the front door and helped Claudia into it. She tucked Claudia's cloak around her. "It will work fine."

"But people are going to stare."

"Let them stare. They will really stare after Jesus heals you, and you start jumping and running." Tirzah tugged on the cart. "Hmm, you are a bit heavier than you used to be."

"Oh, this is ridiculous." Claudia pushed herself up and started to swing her good leg over the edge of the dilapidated wooden cart. "Get me out of here."

"Stay right where you are. Once we get moving it will be easier." Tirzah tugged again, and it grudgingly began to move. "See there. If I can just get it started…"

The trio, Tirzah, Claudia and Sandy, moved through the marketplace amidst the stares of onlookers. Sandy trotted in front as if clearing the way for the two young women, until he saw a stray cat. Then he was off chasing that imminent danger away from his owners.

Tirzah stopped in front of one of the vendor booths they frequented. "Malachi, have you heard whether that man, Jesus, will be in the synagogue today?"

The older bald-headed man with tufts of hair sticking out on the sides above his ears shook his head. "Don't you want some nice eggplant?"

She touched the slight bulge of the few coins in the bag strapped across her shoulder. "Maybe later. We need to find Jesus first."

"I don't know where the man is today." Malachi looked at Claudia in the wagon, then back at Tirzah. He raised his bushy eyebrows and cocked his head.

"Her leg's bothering her today. But not for long." Tirzah tugged on the cart. "Thank you."

Malachi shrugged his shoulders and returned to straightening his colorful fruits and vegetables.

The closer they came to the synagogue, the larger the crowd grew. Tirzah pushed her way through the people pulling the cart behind her. "He must be here." She asked a woman beside her, but the woman pulled her cloak around her and turned her back, muttering, "I don't know."

Tirzah wiped beads of perspiration off her forehead with her scarf. "Does that mean he's not here, or you don't know?"

The woman eyed her suspiciously and jerked her head toward the marketplace. "He's down there."

"Ach! We just came from the marketplace." Tirzah turned the cart around and started back in the direction from which they had come.

Claudia grabbed her arm. "Tirzah, please. Let's just go home. This is too much trouble."

"No, we are going to pursue this…him. If he can't heal you, then we know we did everything we could, but I'm not giving up."

Claudia smiled. "You are very stubborn sometimes, you know."

"So I've been told." The crowd shifted, and Tirzah's gaze latched upon Jesus and his band of followers in the middle of a crowd. "There he is."

Claudia pushed herself up, craning her neck to catch a glimpse of the man. "I can't see him. There are too many people."

Tirzah stood on her tiptoes to see over the clustered crowd. Claudia tugged on her sleeve. "Can you hear him? What's he talking about?"

"Someone named John the Baptist." Tirzah grabbed hold of the wagon handle. She made her way through the gathering, amidst the grumbling and pushing back of the crowd. "Please, I need through. Excuse me, watch the cart."

Claudia ducked her head and closed her eyes, as if she couldn't bear to look up. The unkind comments from the men and women swirled around them. "Whore. Cripple. What are they doing here?"

Tirzah worked her way to the front of the throng and came to a stop in front of the man himself. He rose from where he sat on the edge of a stone wall and came toward her. She was vaguely aware that the noise surrounding them had diminished. Her idea of bringing Claudia to Jesus to be healed seemed silly now, but it was too late to turn back.

His face softened as he smiled at Tirzah. "I saw you yesterday in front of the synagogue."

"Yes."

"Yesterday was for curiosity. Why have you sought me out again today?"

Tirzah turned to Claudia. "My friend. My friend is crippled. All of her life. Born this way." The words she had rehearsed seemed to stick in her mouth. She swallowed and cleared her throat. "I...I believe you can heal her."

She looked back at Jesus, and tears started to trickle down her cheeks. Her lips quivered. "Would you please heal my friend?"

He inclined his head toward Claudia. "Do you wish to be healed?"

Claudia nodded and wiped the tears away that had started down her face as well.

He held his hand out to her. "Give me your hand."

Claudia lifted her good hand toward him.

"No, the other one."

She clutched her withered arm with her good hand.

"Stretch forth the withered arm."

Slowly she brought out the withered arm and hand from the darkness of her cloak. As she raised the deformed limb, it grew, straightened and fleshed out—before their eyes. The young woman gasped.

"Now get up out of that little wagon, my dear woman."

Claudia pulled herself to the edge of the cart and painstakingly swung her legs over. First the good one, then the lame one. Claudia reached for Tirzah, and the two women held hands as Claudia stood slowly, cautiously on two strong, perfect legs. Claudia jerked her head around, her eyes wide, staring at Tirzah.

Claudia placed the healed foot down flat on the ground and took a halting step, gripping Tirzah's hand until her knuckles turned white. Her leg held her up. She took another step—and then another. She walked in a circle around Tirzah, still gripping her friend's hands, testing her new leg. Then she let go and ran around her, Sandy nipping at her heels.

Some of the crowd broke out in laughter. Some murmured. Others gasped in shock. Jesus laughed with them. "Go your way, young lady. Be blessed." He turned to Tirzah, a smile lifting the corners of his mouth. "You

have loved your friend well. Your faith has set her free." He paused. "I suspect I shall see you again soon."

Something like cleansing warm water rushed over and through Tirzah. She stared at Jesus and everything seemed brighter—the blue of the sky, the diverse shades of green in the leaves on the trees, Claudia's eyes, her own hands. A burden lifted from her shoulders—a heretofore unperceived burden. Lightness danced about her, both in what she saw and what she felt.

The crowd pushed in around Jesus, edging the two women to the outer perimeter of the throng. Out of habit, Tirzah grabbed Claudia's arm and began to walk home, pulling the cart behind them.

Claudia was still chuckling to herself. "I don't need you to support me anymore. Look! I can walk on my own. No more limp." She twirled around. The chuckles turned into laughter that bubbled from her throat and filled the air.

That's the most beautiful sound I've ever heard. Tirzah laughed with Claudia as she, the one who had never in her whole life been able to take a step without a limp, danced in the street. The one who had never been able to stretch both arms out together now raised them to the sky.

I saw a miracle today. A true miracle.

chapter 13

Tirzah pulled the empty cart to the courtyard behind the house. Claudia ran up the steps to her quarters, her headpiece flying, then ran down. "Look, Tirzah. I can run up the stairs. I can run!"

Sandy followed Claudia up and down the steps, barking and jumping.

"Be careful, Claudia. Don't trip over the dog. Even sure-footed people fall on stairs." Tirzah held out her hand. "Come here, boy. Leave Claudia alone." She patted the dog's head. "I do believe even he senses something has changed."

Tirzah watched her friend frolic on the steps. The woman had to feel like a completely different person, able to do things she'd never been able to do—walk normally. Hold a cup. Braid her hair. Knot her belt. Put on her shoes. Everyday things physically able people did without thinking.

Tirzah sat on a bench beside the bougainvillea vine that trailed along the wall and reached up to pluck one of the brilliant blossoms. She twirled it between her fingers and then threaded it into her hair. She didn't know how to articulate what she herself was feeling. A shift had occurred in her heart. Her perspective had changed. Everything seemed different somehow and yet the same. She wanted to go back to where Jesus was and listen to

73

his teaching. She wanted to serve him, even if it was only to provide food or water for him and his followers. She wanted to witness more of his miracles firsthand.

The bench toppled over as Tirzah jumped up. "Claudia! We didn't even thank him. We were so excited watching you run and walk, we just rushed away."

Claudia halted near the bottom of the steps. "Oh, dear. How ungrateful of us...me." Her brow furrowed over her coppery eyes that had turned dark. "H...how ungrateful. This has changed my life, and I didn't even say thank you." She whirled around and stepped toward the gate out of the courtyard. "We must go back and find him."

Tirzah caught her by the arm. "Wait. He probably won't be there. Evening is approaching. He will have found someplace for the night. We'll go looking for him again tomorrow."

Brilliant orange and pink rays from the desert sunset cut over the edge of the horizon, casting a bronze glow upon Claudia's face. "Yes, of course, you're right." Claudia looked at Tirzah and touched her hair. "Something's different about you as well, my friend."

Tirzah caught Claudia's hand in her own. "As miraculous as your healing has been, I believe I've had one just as miraculous." Tears formed as she struggled to express the inexpressible. "A miracle in my spirit, my heart." She touched her chest as she spoke.

"Tell me what you mean." Claudia righted the bench and motioned for Tirzah to sit down again.

Tirzah continued to speak as she sat. "I don't know exactly. But when Jesus healed your limbs, and he looked at me, something washed over me—something cleansing and refreshing, like bubbling water, something liberating." Tirzah shook her head. "I can't explain it, but I know I'm different."

Claudia nodded as Tirzah searched for the words to communicate her sentiments. "I understand. It's not just that I am no longer crippled; it's deeper than that." She stood and walked back and forth in front of Tirzah in the growing darkness of the twilight. "When you are crippled physically, the crippling affects the spirit as well. I suppose it shouldn't, but it does. You feel ashamed and inadequate. You sense you are a burden to those around you. You don't feel attractive. But now that Jesus healed my physical body, I feel whole on the inside as well. There's no longer a heaviness on my shoulders." She stopped her pacing and looked at Tirzah. "Am I making any sense?"

"Perfect sense. I am experiencing the same thing." Tirzah stood. "I don't know what precisely has happened to us, but it's almost as if we have a brand new life to live. Before our encounter with Jesus, I was broken—my life, a shattered mess. Even as a little girl I realized my upbringing was not a proper life for a child. All I ever knew was living in the shadows of the disapproval of people and being shuffled through the whispering gossip in the streets. Things simply never felt right to me. I always knew there was a better way. Jesus saw the broken pieces of my life lying scattered on the ground and put them back together. Now...now I feel whole." She stepped back and ran her hands through her hair. "We need to thank him. We shall try to find him again tomorrow."

The two friends came into the house late the next afternoon, exhausted by their search to find Jesus. Claudia sat at the table and took off her headpiece. Tirzah poured two cups of wine. Claudia fingered the edge of her cup. "What shall we do? If Jesus has really gone on to another

village as they said…shall we follow him?"

Tirzah sat with her friend and wiped the perspiration from her forehead with her headpiece that she had removed as well. Her hair hung in ringlets around her face. She shook her head. "I don't think so. I think what we should do is wait until next week. Malachi said he heard Jesus was coming back next week because Simon is holding a banquet in his honor at his house."

Claudia's eyes grew wide. "Your Simon?"

Tirzah chuckled and nodded. "My Simon."

"But we're not invited." Claudia cut a piece of cheese from the round that was on the table and handed it to Tirzah.

Tirzah munched on the chewy morsel. "We don't have to be. We can go early and catch him going in, or we can go in with the gallery of onlookers. It is permitted."

"Oh, dear, I don't know. People here know us. They won't—"

"They won't what? Approve? So what? We don't need their approval. Don't we just want to say thank you?" Tirzah pounded her knee with her fist, punctuating her comments. "We can certainly go and tell the man thank you."

Claudia blinked at her friend's outburst. "Of course."

The realization of how different things were for them was growing in Tirzah's heart. She could no longer work at her mother's profession. Claudia could no longer beg. She didn't know how they would manage, but she knew they had to do something different.

"Claudia, I need to tell you something."

Claudia turned from the shelf where she'd pulled down a stack of bowls. "What is it?" She set the bowls on the table, sat down next to Tirzah, and waited for her to go on.

Tirzah looked down at the wooden table and ran her

fingers along a seam in the wood. She folded her hands on the tabletop. "I cannot work on the streets anymore. Or invite men to…to our…our…"

Claudia eyes reddened with tears. She wiped one away with a quivering finger—a finger that had never functioned properly before.

Tirzah took the now-healed hand in her own. "And you no longer need to beg in the streets."

Claudia drew back and smiled. "I know. What excuse does a whole person have to beg? I believe God is going to provide for us if we trust him."

Tirzah looked at the basket sitting on the table containing a lone onion and a few pieces of garlic. "I don't know how, but I'm hoping he will."

The familiar rap.

Tirzah stood, her pulse thudding in her temples. "Simon. I forgot it was Simon's night." She clutched her cloak in her fists. "What shall I do?"

Claudia started for the door to the courtyard.

"No, wait." Tirzah smoothed her hair. "We shall tell him the truth. I want him to see what has happened to you…to us."

Claudia caught her breath. "He's going to be angry. Maybe we should wait."

"No. There's no need to put this off." She reached for the latch and creaked open the door. "Good evening, Simon. Please come in."

chapter 14

Simon stepped into the room, smiling at Tirzah, the faint familiar cinnamon scent carrying memories of the many nights with this man. His smile melted into a frown as he spotted Claudia. He nodded slightly. "Good evening, ladies." His gaze lingered on Claudia in dismissal. She folded her hands and remained where she stood. An awkward silence ensued as Simon hung his mantle on the customary peg. He cleared his throat. "Are we to have company this evening?"

Tirzah gestured toward the bench at the table. "Sit down, Simon. I have something to tell you—show you." She removed his usual goblet from the shelf and poured a serving of wine into it. She realized that life would never be *usual* again. "Do you notice anything different?"

Simon sat as directed and took a long swig, glaring at Tirzah over the edge of the cup. He looked around the room, ignoring Claudia. He clunked the vessel down, making wine slosh over the edge and onto the table. "No, I see nothing different, except the presence of intrusive company."

Tirzah held out her hand to Claudia. "Come here, dear."

The young woman walked across the room and took Tirzah's hand. Simon leaned back with his hands on his knees. "What is the meaning of this?"

"Look at her, Simon." Tirzah raised Claudia's formerly crippled arm. "Is this a whole, healthy arm?"

Simon stood and walked in a circle around the two women. "What kind of chicanery is this?"

"No chicanery. I took her to the man named Jesus—the man you were questioning last week at the synagogue, the man the whole countryside is in a dither about. He healed her. It's that simple." Tirzah laughed. "Isn't it wonderful?" She twirled Claudia around.

Simon returned to his seat and finished his wine. "I suppose so." He slammed his hand on the table. "Now, could we have some privacy?"

Claudia backed up and turned to leave.

"No, stay." Tirzah faced Simon and clasped her hands in front of her. "Things are not the same, Simon. They will never be the same again. Not only has Claudia been healed of her infirmities, but I have been healed as well—healed of my spiritual infirmity."

Simon stood.

Tirzah took a step backward, but continued to talk. "I can no longer…no longer live like…like this." She walked to the door and opened it. "You must leave and never come back to see me again."

Simon took a step toward her, reached around her, and slammed the door shut. A low rumble began in his belly and came out in a menacing sneer. The full lips she had kissed so often turned grim and flat. Tirzah's knees wobbled as rage exploded from Simon. "If you think you can dismiss me this easily, you have another thing coming." He grabbed Tirzah around the throat and lifted her up, slamming her against the wall. Her head hit the wall with a sickening clunk. His face reddened as his grip tightened, choking the breath from her. Beads of sweat broke out on his forehead and dripped onto her face. She struggled for

air and flailed at his face with her hands. Inky black edged her vision as her fingers found a target and drew blood from his cheeks.

Claudia screamed and lunged at him, pounding him on the back with both fists. "Stop it! You're killing her! Stop it!" Guttural gasps escaped from Tirzah's throat as she struggled for breath.

Outside, Sandy jumped against the door, scratching on it and barking, but he could not gain entrance.

Simon was too strong for the women. Panicked, Claudia darted to the woodpile and picked up a log. She pulled it over her shoulder and swung it at Simon with all of her newfound strength, striking him in the middle of his back. The blow caused his knees to buckle and his grip on Tirzah to loosen. She slumped to the floor, half conscious, wheezing for air.

Simon let go of Tirzah and turned toward Claudia. She raised the log again and spoke in a low but firm, steady tone. "You'll leave now, sir. And you will never come back."

Raising his hands and backing away, Simon shook his head. "I...I don't know what came over me." He gathered his cloak from the peg beside the door. He pointed his blunt, stodgy finger at Tirzah. "Don't worry, you slut. I'll never darken your door again." He spat his words out in an ominous whisper. "We'll see how well you survive without my support if you're no longer active in your—" He scoffed. "—your profession." He wiped his bloody cheek with the back of his hand, knotted his belt and walked out the door, slamming it behind him.

Claudia dropped the log and ran to Tirzah, who was on her knees, struggling to get up. "Are you...can you breathe?"

Tirzah put up her hand. "I...I think so. Give me a moment." Her voice came out raspy and hoarse. She

coughed and got to her feet with Claudia's support. "I find
it hard to believe that kind of rage came from him." She
looked at Claudia and smiled. "Now you're helping me."

Claudia poured Tirzah a cup of wine and held her arm
as she sat down. "Here, sip this. It will help."

Tirzah encircled the goblet with trembling fingers.
"Thank you, friend." She took a sip and touched her throat.
"Oh…that hurts."

"I'm sorry. I wish I could do something to help."

"What do you mean? You saved my life. If you hadn't
been here, he would have killed me, just like my mother
was…" Tirzah's voice trailed off, and she took another sip
of wine.

Claudia looked at her hands. "If I hadn't been healed, I
would have been useless to help you."

Tirzah smirked. "If *I* hadn't been healed, you wouldn't
have had to."

A long silence hung between the two—the kind of
silence that would be awkward between individuals
who didn't know each other well, but which was entirely
comfortable between those who knew each other's
intimate thoughts and feelings.

Tirzah broke the hush of the moment. "Do you want
to sleep downstairs tonight?" She indicated the little
alcove that had been hers as a child. "It's small, but you are
welcome to sleep there."

"I think I'd like to go back on the roof to my room."
She shrugged her shoulders. "I like going up and down the
steps so easily."

"I understand. I…I simply…" Tirzah's eyes filled with
moisture. "I don't want to be alone tonight."

Claudia reached for her friend and touched her arm.
"Oh, of course. I'll go up for my things and be back shortly."
She took a step toward the door then turned to her friend.

"Don't worry, my friend. I don't know how God will do it, but I know he is faithful and will take care of us."

Tirzah could not sleep that night. The pain in her throat awakened her every time she swallowed. Even sipping the wine didn't help. She was glad to see the soft glow of dawn across the eastern sky. She lit a lantern and peered at her neck in the bronze looking glass. Angry red marks were visible even in the dim light. Throwing on her clothes, she went to the oven to stir the embers into an active flame. There was a chill in the air this morning. She started outside with a bucket to milk the goat.

"I'll do that." Claudia came out from the alcove, tucking her cloak into her belt. "That's something I've never been able to help you with before. Now I can." She smiled shyly at Tirzah. "You're up early this morning."

Tirzah rubbed her throat. "I didn't sleep very well."

"No wonder. Let me look at those marks." Claudia tilted Tirzah's head to the side in the early morning light from the window. "Hmm. Those are nasty looking. Sit down and let's put some hyssop on them." She went to a cabinet in the corner and removed a small vial, uncorked it, and poured the thick oil into the palm of her hand. "Aunt Dorcas would rub this in between my fingers on my crippled hand when they chafed from rubbing together. It might sting a bit at first, but it will soothe the wounds." She applied the ointment and rubbed it into the contusions that had turned blue and purple overnight. "How does that feel?"

Tirzah nodded. "It's fine. Thank you." She stretched her neck and massaged it. "You are a dear friend."

Claudia replaced the cork on the vial and picked up

the bucket. "I shall be back shortly with a pail full of milk."

"Hmm. There's a bit of a trick to the milking, but you'll get the hang of it."

"I've watched often enough."

Sandy stood at the door waiting to be let out, his tail wagging enthusiastically. Claudia snapped her fingers. "C'mon boy. A new day to thank God for."

A knock came on the door, startling the two women. Tirzah put her hand on Claudia's knee and rose. "Who would be at our door this early?"

"What if it is Simon?"

Tirzah went to the door. "I don't think so. I don't think he will ever come back." She put her ear to the door. "Who is it?"

chapter 15

"Malachi."

"Malachi?" Tirzah opened the door to their friend. He stood in the doorway holding in each hand a basket full of fruit and vegetables—melons, cucumbers, mangos, grapes, dates, figs, onions, honey, lentils.

"Could you use these? I had so much left over from the market yesterday, much more than we need, so I thought… well, I mean, if you don't want them, it's fine, but I just thought perhaps you might need some extra food."

"My goodness! How did you happen to have this much surplus, Malachi?" Tirzah opened the door and motioned for him to come in.

Malachi shook his head and waved her off. "No, no thank you."

Of course, the man would not enter a harlot's house. How had she forgotten? Her thinking had already made the switch. In her heart she was no longer a prostitute.

"Uh, I do not know—not as many customers for some reason. I purchased too much. I don't know, but you're welcome to what I have here if you'd like it." He scratched his bald head. "It will spoil if I try to keep it." He brushed dirt from a melon. "Can you use it?"

Tirzah started laughing, and Claudia joined her amusement. Malachi looked from one to the other. "What is so funny?" He shuffled his feet. "I must get to my shop.

I'll just leave this here. If you cannot use it, give it to someone else." He started to leave then turned around and looked at Claudia. "Something's different about you."

"Indeed there is." She whirled around in a circle. "The man named Jesus healed me. Look." She held her healed arm up in the air and waved at the man.

"Well! Well, now! I hardly know what to say. That's… that's a…"

"A miracle?" The two women nodded. "We would agree." Tirzah stepped toward Malachi. "Do you know where Jesus went when he left Capernaum?"

"I heard he went into the countryside with his followers but will be back. I told you about the banquet to be held at Simon's house."

"When is it exactly?"

"In two days is what I heard." Malachi backed away. "I must take my leave. Good day, ladies." Then the man hurried from their door, glancing from side to side, leaving not only the food, but the baskets too.

They each picked up a basket and lugged them into the house. Tirzah picked through the produce. "Hmm, some are overripe and have bad spots, but we can salvage most of it. We'll make a large pot of stew with the lentils, onions, and peppers. Dry the fruit. We can eat for days on this."

Claudia joined Tirzah in sorting through the baskets and smiled. "I knew God would provide."

"Hmm. I agree, but we cannot expect Malachi to come to our door every day with surplus like this from his shop, can we?"

"No, however I believe God will find a way if we'll trust him. One never knows what God is going to do."

Tirzah wiped her hands on a towel and went back to work on the food. "I must admit I certainly didn't plan on something like this, that's for sure. Perhaps God *is* going

to take care of us."

Tirzah watched Claudia and Sandy go out to do the milking in the thin, early morning sunlight. Feeling weak, she sat down for a moment. *How can I ever thank God for what he has done for us? I could have been dead. Claudia could still be crippled.* As she tossed the bad fruit and vegetables in a pot to take out to feed the goat and the good pieces either into the stew or on a stone to be dried, Tirzah thought about the upcoming banquet at Simon's house. There would be lavish food and many servants. And likely there would be an abundance of guests.

Claudia came in with the pail about half full of milk. "I see what you mean—not as easy as it looks, but I got half a pail. Enough for today."

Tirzah stood and gesturing with a knife in her hand as she spoke. "I really do want to see Jesus again. I want to thank him. I want to learn from him. I simply want to be around him." She sliced a ripe melon with a swift downward motion. "We are going to that banquet. We can go just like everybody else."

Claudia took Sandy and went upstairs to her quarters on the roof.

Tirzah watched Claudia leave and sighed. *That's fine and good Malachi happened to have extra produce today, but what happens next week and then the next? How are we going to survive with neither one of us…working? No money? What about money to pay the landlord?*

What am I doing? Am I praying? Tirzah didn't really know the proper words to pray, but her thoughts seemed directed to God.

Trust me.

Tirzah shook her head. *That's just me, my own thoughts. I've resorted to talking to myself.*

Trust me.

She added water to the kettle of chopped vegetables and hung it over the fire. Despite her skepticism, Tirzah sensed a burgeoning faith in her heart—a trust, a belief that God cared for them. She began the routine of grinding enough grain to bread flour—a process fixed in her from years of repetition. After she finished, she would have to go see the landlord. *How is God going to pay our rent?* She looked at her hands now kneading the dough. *I could take him some bread. Perhaps he would accept that in partial payment.* But even though he was a widower, he had servants to attend to all his needs. She reached for the honey Malachi had brought them. Perhaps he would like some sweet bread. She dribbled it into the dough.

Claudia had returned and was stirring the kettle of stew. "Smells wonderful."

Tirzah put the loaves of dough into the clay oven. Wiping her hands on a towel, she sat at the table. "I must go see the landlord today. We are behind on rent." She wiped the perspiration from her forehead. "I'm surprised he hasn't sent his servant to collect."

"Do you feel strong enough to go? Are you concerned?" Claudia tasted the liquid from the stew. "I'm going to add some cumin."

"That will taste good." Tirzah folded her hands in her lap. "I'm fine. And am I concerned?" She reached down and scratched Sandy behind his ears. "I find myself in quite a conundrum. I feel I should be concerned, but a spirit of peace and calm keeps pushing the concern aside."

"I'm experiencing the same thing." Claudia sat facing Tirzah. "It has to be God, but I don't know how to explain it. A spirit of well-being has invaded my heart."

Tirzah stood and hung the towel on a wall hook. "Would you mind the bread? I'm going to freshen up. Then I'll take one of the loaves with me to visit with the

landlord. Perhaps he will have mercy on us."

Tirzah went to her room to wash and change her cloak. She wound her hair in a knot and put a headdress over it. No more wearing her hair loose as did the harlots. She would no longer signal men with her loose-flowing locks. Suddenly from a place hidden deep within her, tears of gratitude flowed. Waves of emotion billowed from her soul. She was no longer a woman stained by the scourge of prostitution. She felt clean, spotless, pristine. How was that possible? She looked into her bronze mirror. Wiping the tears away, she stared at her image. Her eyes were bloodshot and the red marks around her throat visible, but her face appeared shining and innocent. She buried her face in her hands and wept anew.

"Tirzah?" Claudia's soft voice called to her. She stood at the archway into Tirzah's room. "What distresses you?"

Tirzah brushed the tears away and reached for her friend. She smiled. "It is the opposite, actually. My heart overflows with gratitude for something I do not comprehend. I do not know everything our encounter with Jesus accomplished, but it was much more than your physical healing." She twisted a handkerchief in her hands. "I feel like a little girl again. I must think of some way to express that gratitude to him. We will proceed with plans to attend the banquet at Simon's house, but first..." Tirzah rose and tied her sash. "First I need to face our landlord."

She wrapped up a fresh loaf of bread Claudia had just removed from the oven and put it in a basket. "I shall not be gone long." She looked around the small house where she had grown up. If the landlord didn't show her mercy, he could order them to vacate that very day. She may have to say good-bye forever to the only home she had ever known.

chapter 16

Tirzah hurried down the street through the marketplace to the elegant residence of their landlord on the outskirts of the village. Ordinarily, a collector sat at the gate taking monies from his various tenants, mostly vineyard keepers. A grizzled old man with most of his teeth missing did the collecting for years, but recently a younger man had taken over the responsibility. She supposed it was perhaps one of Nahash's sons. When she was a child, Tirzah took their house for granted—the "arrangement," her mother called it. But after Rhoda died and Nahash grew older, the "arrangement" was no longer an option. Tirzah had to start paying rent.

However, today no one was in sight. The collection table was not set up. Tirzah took a deep breath and pulled the bell at the entrance. No servant answered. She looked through the gate. No servants scurrying back and forth. No chatter or activity at all. She walked around the wall to the back, still not seeing anyone. Returning to the gate and not being able to rouse a soul, she walked down the street to the nearest shop.

Joshua, a small man with beady eyes, stood at the entrance plying his wares to shoppers as they passed by. He held several strands of beads in his hands. "Want some nice beads today, lady?" He thrust the necklaces out toward her. "Oh, it's you, Tirzah. I didn't recognize you.

What are you doing out this time of day?" He spat toward her feet. "You look different."

"I *am* different." She didn't wish to go into an explanation, so she pointed toward her landlord's residence. "Where is Nahash? The place looks deserted."

"Didn't you know?" The shopkeeper pointed to a tray. "How about some new bracelets?"

Tirzah shook her head. "Know what? What about Nahash?"

"Moved his whole household into the country a couple of weeks ago. Said he would send someone back to collect debts, but as of yet, no one has shown up."

"What about our rent? He's your landlord as well, isn't he?"

The shopkeeper shot her a lecherous glance and snickered. "Yes, but my place doesn't see near the action that I'm sure yours does." His shoulders shook with forced laughter.

Tirzah glared at him. "I said I'm different, and I truly am. I don't...don't do that anymore." She held his gaze. "I simply want to talk to him about my rent."

"Mm, yes, well..." The man wiped his nose with his sleeve. "Don't worry about it until you hear from him. He'll get in touch with you when he returns to settle up."

Tirzah took a step back. "There's nothing to be done then?"

"Not now." He looked at the basket. "Smells like fresh bread."

"Would you like some? I bake delicious bread."

"I know you do. Remember, I used to purchase from you before you...you started..." He cleared his throat. "Yes, I'd like to purchase that loaf."

"No, it's my gift to you." Tirzah took it out of the basket and held it out for the man.

The man raised his eyebrows. "Really? That's very generous of you."

"Think nothing of it." She turned to go.

"Wait, Tirzah. Please forgive me. I was rude." He swept his hand over his trays of goods. "We all do what we have to in order to survive, don't we?"

Tirzah stared at the man. "Thank you. Let me know when Nahash returns."

She returned home with the empty basket. *Our landlord has moved? That's how God is going to provide for us? No one around to pay rent to? This is a strange way to provide for someone—the absence of a bill collector. And all of this because of an encounter with a man who healed my heart? I don't understand this, God, but I'm grateful.*

Claudia's eyes widened in disbelief as Tirzah shared the news of the missing landlord with her. They laughed and danced a jig in the middle of the room, giggling like they were little girls once again. Tirzah was determined more than ever to get to Simon's banquet.

The day of the banquet arrived. The two women went about their daily chores. Claudia milked the goat then prepared their morning meal. Tirzah ground the flour and baked the bread. Later in the day after trying to keep busy to make the day pass quicker, Tirzah told Claudia, "It's time. Go upstairs and dress. I want to arrive at Simon's house early."

"Yes, I won't take long." Claudia hurried out the door, and Tirzah heard her ascend the steps without the clomp-clomp of her former limp to her quarters on the roof, which she had not slept in since they met Jesus last week. Tirzah still did not want to be alone downstairs at night.

She went to her chest of clothing and removed her best tunic, embroidered with red tapestry ribbon, and her finest cloak. *After all, we are going to a banquet.*

She finished dressing and put on a pair of gold bangle earrings and donned matching bracelets. She wound her hair in a knot, securing it with a pin, and pulled the headpiece over her hair. The crown Adam had sent winked at her from its place on the wall as rays from the late afternoon sun glimmered through the strands of gold. Tirzah stared at it. She let the headpiece down around her shoulders and removed the crown from its resting place on the wall peg. Donning the circlet, she looked in the bronze mirror, then she pushed it back on her head and pulled her headpiece into place. Taking another look, she was satisfied that the casual onlooker would not be able to detect the crown, but she wanted to wear it. For the first time in her life, she truly felt like a princess.

She walked out of her room and opened the door. "Claudia, are you ready?"

"Be right down."

Sandy bounded down the stairs and into the house. His tail wagged his body as he looked up at Tirzah. She laughed and ruffled the fur on his head. "No, boy. You cannot go with us this time." The dog walked to the hearth and lay down with his head resting on his paws. He blinked at Tirzah and whined. Tirzah knelt beside the faithful animal and nuzzled his head with her cheek. "Not today." She stood as Claudia came into the room.

She wore her best garments as well, a bronze tunic and cloak that highlighted her eyes. "You look beautiful, Tirzah."

"So do you." She pointed to the dog watching the two women. "Sandy's making his appeal to go with us. Look at those sad eyes."

Claudia laughed and gave the dog a pat. "This is a festive affair only for humans, I'm afraid." She embraced Tirzah. Taking a step backward, she touched Tirzah's arm. "You are trembling. Are you nervous?"

"I suppose I am, but I'm eager as well." She started for the door, then hesitated and went to a wooden cabinet. Opening it, she removed the alabaster jar that Simon had given her just a few nights ago.

"What are you going to do with that?"

Tirzah turned the jar around in her hands. "I…it's the most valuable item I own. I just want to give Jesus a gift."

"Didn't Simon give that to you?"

Tirzah nodded.

"Oo." Claudia's voice inflection went from high to low. "That is going to upset him to know that you are giving away a gift he gave you—and such a valuable one at that."

"He won't see it. I'll give it to Jesus on his way in…or perhaps on his way out."

Claudia let Sandy out into the courtyard, then went to the front door to unlatch it. "I don't know. I think Simon's already going to be angry when he sees us. To further anger him by giving away an expensive gift to someone that he is leery of to begin with—"

"Oh, pshaw!" Tirzah flicked her wrist at Claudia. "You worry too much. Simon probably won't even notice us in the crowd." She tucked the jar into a pocket in her tunic. She crisscrossed her cloak and tied a colorful sash to secure the opening. "Let's go. I cannot wait to see Jesus again. I have a sense this day is pivotal for us."

chapter 17

A mass of people had gathered outside Simon's house by the time the two women arrived. Tirzah inquired of a bystander, "Has Jesus arrived?"

Without looking, a woman on the edge of the crowd answered, "Not yet." Then she faced Tirzah. "Oh. People like you are not welcome at an occasion such as this."

The familiar whispers started. "What is she doing here?"

"Whore."

"Harlot."

Tirzah's heart raced and thudded against her chest. She grabbed Claudia's arm. "I will not be turned away. Follow me. I know how to get into the courtyard the back way." She scoffed and muttered underneath her breath, "Past experience is worth something, I suppose."

Tirzah led Claudia around the outside wall of the residence, then they slipped through a back gate and took their place along with the other spectators on the inside of the wall. The sumptuous banquet had been set in place in the traditional "U" arrangement. Luxurious pillows in every color imaginable lined the outside of the low table on which the invited guests reclined after they entered. The smoky scent of roasted meat floated through the air. Tirzah swallowed as her mouth watered. Her tender throat reminded her of Simon's horrific attack on her a mere few hours before.

The pair stationed themselves behind a large potted plant where they could observe without being seen. Simon, the hospitable host that he always was, greeted his guests with the customary kiss, washing of dust from sandaled feet, and anointing of the guests' head with oil. Tirzah glanced around the courtyard and recognized most of the faces. There were ordinarily many women among the spectators, but today there seemed to be more than the usual number of men. Tirzah assumed it was in anticipation of Jesus' attendance. A murmur spread through the crowd. Tirzah's breath quickened. "There he is. He's here."

Heads turned toward the entrance as Jesus and his followers walked into the courtyard. People immediately gathered around him, making it difficult for him to get to the banquet table. He chatted with one person after another. Placing his hand on a shoulder, nodding in response to comments. Finally his group took their places. Tirzah stared—appalled at the proceedings. Simon had not greeted Jesus properly. He did not give him the traditional kiss. He had not instructed the servants to wash his feet. No oil for his head.

Where was Simon? She spotted him on the opposite side of the garden with his back to Jesus and his party. He swiveled his head and looked her way, but she stepped behind a pillar. "Claudia, did Simon see me?"

"I don't think so. He's showing some of his colleagues where to be seated." She looked again. "Food is being served."

Tirzah peeked around the pillar at Jesus. He had reclined at the table and was conversing with one of his followers. Her cheeks burned at the ill treatment of Jesus. He should have been the most honored guest. Her heart

felt like it was going to leap from her throat, but she took a deep breath, stepped forward, and walked toward him. Comments followed her.

"What is she doing?"

"Somebody stop her."

"This is disgraceful."

"Get her out of here."

She stopped and knelt at the feet of Jesus, looking up at him. He turned, leaned up on his elbow, and smiled in recognition. Sobs, unrestrained, rose soundlessly from Tirzah's belly and caught in her throat. "I...I wanted to thank you. We...". She inclined her head toward Claudia, still standing in the shadows of the gallery. "We left the other day without...without thanking you." She dissolved in a sob and buried her face in her hands. Hot tears coursed down her cheeks to seep through her fingers. She raised her tear-stained face. "It wasn't only my friend who was healed of her infirmity that afternoon, but something inside of me was healed as well. I am no longer the same. I am so grateful."

Her tears trickled down and fell on his dusty feet. "Oh, oh dear. I'm so sorry." She tried to wipe the tears from his feet with her hands. She looked about for a towel, but not seeing one, pulled her headpiece down, and unwound her hair. Tirzah heard the gasps around her, but a lifetime of ignoring the spurns of people had desensitized her. Feeling the crown that held her hair back, she removed it and lay it down. She caught her hair in her hands and wiped the tears away with the thick tresses as she tried to subdue her weeping. But the more she struggled to stop her tears, the harder they flowed. She reached into her tunic and pulled out the alabaster jar. Almost in one motion she broke off the top and poured the fragrant ointment on Jesus's feet. The aroma wound its way around the courtyard, filling the atmosphere.

Tirzah bent forward and kissed his feet over and over. "Thank you, thank you, thank you." A hush fell on the gathering—no audible sound except Tirzah's sobs.

Simon approached, saying nothing. The scowl on his face said it all. Jesus looked at the man and directed his attention to him. "Simon, I have something to say to you."

"Say it, Teacher."

Jesus sat up as he spoke. "Two men were in debt to a banker. One owed five hundred silver pieces, the other fifty. Neither of them could pay up, and so the banker canceled both debts. Which of the two would be more grateful?"

Simon answered, "I suppose the one who was forgiven the most."

"That's right," said Jesus. Then turning to Tirzah, but still speaking to Simon, he said, "Do you see this woman? I came to your home; you provided no water for my feet, but she rained tears on my feet and dried them with her hair. You gave me no greeting, but from the time I arrived she hasn't quit kissing my feet. You provided nothing for freshening up, but she has soothed my feet with perfume. Impressive, isn't it? She was forgiven many sins, and so she is very grateful. If the forgiveness is minimal, the gratitude is minimal."

Then he spoke to Tirzah, "Your sins are forgiven."

Tirzah rose and wiped her eyes with her headpiece as she put it back on. The place was abuzz with comments from the dinner guests. "Who does he think he is, forgiving sins?"

"Ignore them." Jesus smiled. "And don't forget your crown."

"I want to leave that for you. It's my most prized possession."

He leaned over, picked it up, and handed it to her. "You keep it for now, to remind you that you are a princess."

Tirzah's eyes grew wide. "How did you…?"

He put his finger to his lips. "Shh. One day in the Kingdom you will be able to lay all of your crowns at my feet. But for now, you keep this one."

Tirzah looked back at Claudia, who was now standing in front of the plant, tears running down her face. Jesus nodded to her. "You too, Claudia. Go and be blessed."

Turning back to Tirzah, he said, "Your faith has saved you. Go in peace."

chapter 18

Tirzah picked up the crown and rose to her feet. Simon glared at her as she walked past him to leave. His glares went unacknowledged. She took Claudia's arm, and the dinner guests parted as the pair moved toward the entrance—the front entrance—their heads held high, ignoring the whispers. The heady fragrance of the ointment followed them as they exited into the slanted rays of the late afternoon sun. Neither of the women spoke, stunned by what had just occurred.

"Tirzah!"

Tirzah whirled around at the sound of the familiar voice. A man ran toward her with arms outstretched.

"Adam?"

The now mature, but still handsome man picked the young woman up and swung her around. "You're a bit bigger than the last time I did that."

Tirzah threw her arms around his neck. "Adam, is it really you? What are you doing here?" She backed up and held on to his hands, searching his dark eyes for the acceptance that she had seen in those eyes years before—the love. What had been in them when she was a little girl was still there.

He took a deep breath. "My business brings me here once a year. Through the years every time I came I considered visiting you and your mother, but I never did."

He rubbed his beard. "I suppose I knew it would be a terrible temptation for me to be with you all once again." Adam's eyes grew sad, and he sighed. "I'm so sorry. I sent money from time to time…and gifts."

"I know." Tirzah chuckled and held up the crown. "This was my favorite." She laughed and twirled around, placing the crown back on her head.

"Ah, yes. I remember that…Princess." He kissed Tirzah's hands and caressed her dimple with the back of his fingers, just as he used to do. "Can you ever forgive me?"

Tirzah tossed a look toward Simon's courtyard. "Oh, Adam. I've just been forgiven of the most grievous of sins. That man, Jesus, has come from God to set us all free. Free! I see that now. Of course, I forgive you." She hugged him once again. "My friend, Claudia, here. She was a cripple Jesus miraculously healed just a few days ago."

Adam looked at Claudia with raised eyebrows. "Is that a fact? I've been hearing rumors about him. That's the reason I accepted the invitation to the banquet. I was curious about this man. So he is genuine?"

Claudia smiled and spun around. "It is true. And I am so happy to finally meet you."

Tirzah brushed at her eyes as tears threatened to gather again. "Oh, dear. This is all a bit overwhelming."

"What about your mother? Is she well?"

"Mother's gone." Tirzah rubbed her forehead. "It was terrible. Claudia and I had to bury her."

Adam patted her hand. "I'm so sorry. I didn't know." He shifted his weight. "When I heard the commotion from where I was seated at the banquet table, and then I saw the hair, that rich mahogany color, I knew it was you." He brushed a lock of her hair from her cheek. "I was frozen to my spot." His voice grew thick with emotion. "I watched you pour your heart out as the oil poured over his feet. Watching you was wrenching, beautiful, embarrassing, compelling—all of those emotions combined into a confusing swirl. I wanted to rescue you, but something prevented me." Adam's eyes reddened as he spoke.

"It was something I had to do. It was God who held you in your place." Tirzah looked around. "Let's go to the house. I have much to tell you. Can you do that? Do you have a horse, a donkey? Where are you staying?"

The corner of Adam's mouth turned up in his characteristic grin. "My caravan is just down at the inn. I walked here. Yes, let's go to your house." They started toward Tirzah's house, the three of them arm in arm. "Are you…did you get…do you have a husband?"

Tirzah shook her head. "No. I had no dowry, no one to negotiate and arrange a marriage for me." She looked up at Adam. "I always thought you would come back and rescue me."

"Well, I am here to rescue you now. A little late, perhaps, but here I am. My wife is a virtuous woman and knows all about you. She was concerned about your…situation. In fact, she encouraged me to come back and find you. Although I have children of my own, I've always thought of you as a daughter." He took her hand and kissed it. "Would you do me the honor of becoming a part of our family?"

"Oh, a family. A real family? Do you really mean that?" Tirzah stopped. "You are not late. If you'd come any sooner, I wouldn't have met Jesus."

Claudia had fallen behind Adam and Tirzah as they chatted. Tirzah motioned to her. "Come, my dear friend." She took Claudia's hands and looked at Adam. "I will happily join your family…if Claudia is welcome too."

"Hmm." He stroked his beard that now had a sprinkling

of gray hairs here and there. "I hadn't considered two new daughters." Claudia's long lashes brushed her cheeks as she looked down. "But I suppose that would be fine. My wife is a wonderfully generous woman. We have a large estate. I'm sure she would agree." He threw back his head and laughed. "You all will fit in well with our five daughters." He added, "We have two sons as well."

They resumed walking. As they approached the house, Tirzah stopped again. "There's one more member of the family that I need to tell you about." Her tone had turned serious.

"Oh? A child?"

Tirzah and Claudia giggled. "In a way."

Tirzah touched Adam's arm. "You actually have met this member of our family before."

"I have?"

Tirzah put her hand on the latch. "Sandy is going to be very happy to see you once more."

DISCUSSION QUESTIONS

- Through the years scholars have debated whether there were one, two or even three anointings of Jesus. I have taken my story primarily from the Luke 7:36-50 passage which scholars believe took place early in his ministry. In John 12:1-3 we have the account of Mary of Bethany anointing Jesus's feet shortly before his crucifixion. Then in Mark 14:1-3 and Matthew 26:6-7 are accounts of perhaps another anointing. Compare and contrast these passages, and decide for yourself how many anointings you think took place.

- It is so interesting to me that the woman in this beloved story in Luke remains unnamed, and yet because of her courage to express her love and worship to Jesus, her story has touched millions. What about this story touches you the most? Her courage to defy the culture to express her love for Jesus? Her brokenness? Her extravagance? Her changed life? Her faith? Give a reason for your answer.

- Extravagant love calls for extravagant expression. Tirzah expressed her extravagant love for Jesus in extravagant worship which caused derision and ridicule. David expressed his extravagant worship for God by dancing with all his might in front of the ark and the people of God, which produced scornful remarks from his own wife. In what ways have you expressed your love for Jesus in worship? Are they extravagant or more subdued? Does it matter as long as the heart is sincere?

- Has there ever been a time when you have gone against the grain of culture or tradition to do what you felt God wanted you to do? What happened?

- Had you ever thought about the fact that this woman

must have gone to Simon's house intentionally to carry out this act? Otherwise she most probably would not have had the oil with her. I had not thought about it until I started writing. That the alabaster box was a gift from one of her customers came early to me as I outlined the plot. What are some other possibilities of where the costly oil came from? What is the most costly gift you have given to the Lord?

- I've seen many pictures of this occasion and most of them are incorrect. The alabaster box couldn't simply be uncapped in order to pour out the ointment. She had to break the vial and pour it all out. What do you think the broken vial represents? What do you think the fragrant oil represents?

- Relate the story to this Scripture in 2 Corinthians 2:15-16. I believe the fragrance of that ointment filled the banquet hall, touching everyone present. What was the fragrance to the bystanders? To Simon?

- What do you think your response would have been if you'd been present at the banquet at Simon's house? What is your response to the passage today?

Let me invite you to lavish extravagant worship on Jesus today, whether in your private quiet time, in your small group in this Bible study or the next time you go to worship service at your church. He loves us extravagantly. Shouldn't we worship Him in kind?

Don't miss the other titles in the
Hidden Faces Series

Trapped: The Adulterous Woman
Available now!

Alone: The Woman at the Well
Available now!

Hopeless: The Woman with the Issue of Blood
Coming April 2014

And the compilation
of all 4 novellas
Hidden Faces: Portraits of Namelss Women in the Gospels

If you enjoyed *Trapped*, you may also enjoy
these other titles from WhiteFire Publishing.

Shadowed in Silk
by Christine Lindsay

She was invisible to those who should
have loved her.

Dance of the Dandelion
by Dina L. Sleiman

Love's quest leads her the world over.

Jewel of Persia
by Roseanna M. White

How can she love the king of kings
without forsaking her Lord of lord?

A Stray Drop of Blood
by Roseanna M. White

One little drop to soil her garment.
One little drop to cleanse her soul.

Walks Alone
by Sandi Rog

A Cheyenne warrior bent on vengeance.
A pioneer woman bent on fulfilling a dream.
UNTIL THEIR PATHS COLLIDE.